**She must ha[ve]
for treating [... with]
indifference.**

Ben couldn't prevent a wry smile from curling his lips as he considered his present unenviable situation. Had he truly been a groom, born and bred to the life, he would probably have accepted his young mistress's indifference to his presence without so much as a blink. But he was Sharnbrook, with proud aristocratic blood flowing through his veins, and he'd be damned if he would tolerate being ignored by the young woman who was destined to become his Duchess!

The instant she glimpsed that tall figure looming alongside, Sophia could feel the tension in her steadily mounting. How could she now begin to treat this man like a servant when she had never done so before? Impossible to tell him to remember his station in life when she herself was finding it increasingly difficult not to think of him as an equal!

**A young woman disappears.
A husband is suspected of murder.
Stirring times for all the neighbourhood in**

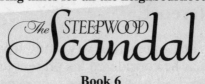

The STEEPWOOD
Scandal

Book 6

When the debauched Marquis of Sywell won
Steepwood Abbey years ago at cards, it led to the death
of the then Earl of Yardley. Now he's caused scandal
again by marrying a girl out of his class—and young
enough to be his granddaughter! After being married
only a short time, the Marchioness has disappeared,
leaving no trace of her whereabouts. There is every
expectation that yet more scandals will emerge, though
no one yet knows just how shocking they will be.

The four villages surrounding the Steepwood Abbey
estate are in turmoil, not only with the dire goings-on
at the Abbey, but also with their own affairs. Each
story in **The Steepwood Scandal** follows the mystery
behind the disappearance of the young woman, and the
individual romances of lovers connected in some way
with the intrigue.

**Regency Drama
intrigue, mischief...and marriage**

A NOBLE MAN

Anne Ashley

*First published in Great Britain 2001
Harlequin Mills & Boon Limited,
Eton House, 18-24 Paradise Road, Richmond, Surrey TW9 1SR*

© Harlequin Books S.A. 2001

Special thanks and acknowledgement are given to Anne Ashley
for her contribution to The Steepwood Scandal series.

ISBN 0 263 82847 6

*Set in Times Roman 10½ on 12½ pt.
119-1001-58697*

*Printed and bound in Spain
by Litografia Rosés S.A., Barcelona*

Anne Ashley was born and educated in Leicester. She lived for a time in Scotland, but now resides in the West Country with two cats, her two sons and a husband who has a wonderful and very necessary sense of humour. When not pounding away at the keys of her computer she likes to relax in her garden, which she has opened to the public on more than one occasion in aid of the village church funds.

Look out for
LORD EXMOUTH'S INTENTIONS
by Anne Ashley

in **The Steepwood Scandal**
Coming Soon

TO NORTHAMPTON

LONDON ROAD

ABBOT QUINCEY

GILES WOOD

NORTH

ABBOT GILES

THE ABBEY

LITTLE STEEP RIVER

STEEP ABBOT

DAM

LAKE

STEEP WOOD

STEEP RIDE

STEEP RIVER

MAP OF STEEPWOOD ABBEY AND DISTRICT 1811 - 1812

ROADS

FOOTPATHS

BY-WAYS

RIVER

DRIVE

Chapter One

March 1812

The Earl of Yardley glared in frustrated silence at his daughter's lustrous blue-black curls. Anyone might be forgiven for supposing that Lady Sophia's bent head and clasped hands expressed contrition, but he was not fooled for a moment. Oh, most definitely not! Unless he much mistook the matter, his daughter's striking green eyes were twinkling while she was doing her level best to conceal that wickedly provocative smile of hers.

'So, you flatly refuse even to consider this latest proposal,' he reiterated, still somehow managing to keep a tight rein on his temper. Any other young woman would have been overjoyed to receive four offers for her hand since her arrival in town a mere two weeks ago. His Sophia, however, was a law unto herself!

Swinging round on his heels, he went across the room to stare sightlessly out of the library window. 'At least may I be permitted to know why you have taken Lord Vale in such dislike?'

'Oh, I do not dislike him, Papa,' his most undutiful offspring hurriedly assured him. 'The truth of the matter is I haven't known him long enough to form an opinion.'

'In that case, what can be your objection other than a need to know him a little better?'

Sophia, with a suspicion of wicked amusement still lingering in her eyes after learning of this latest offer for her hand, raised her head at last. 'Well, apart from the fact that he will never see forty again, he is the only gentleman of my acquaintance who could sit in a carriage and stare out of both windows at one and the same time.'

A noise sounding suspiciously like a suppressed chuckle reached her ears, and she looked across the room at her father's surprisingly straight back and silver-grey hair. For a gentleman who had celebrated his seventy-first birthday just a few short weeks before, he was still in fine physical condition. 'Papa, you don't seriously expect me to consider this offer from Lord Vale, do you?'

He didn't, but he had no intention of admitting to it. 'You seem to forget that I was several years older than Lord Vale is now when I proposed to your mother.'

'True, but you were such a distinguished-looking

gentleman…still are, for that matter. Besides which, you haven't a turn in your left eye.'

'Don't try those wheedling ways with me, my girl!' his lordship snapped, striving not to let his favourite child twist him round her little finger, which, sadly, she so often did. 'Very well, I can understand your reluctance in not wishing to consider Vale's offer, but what about the one from young Farley?'

Sophia's finely arched brows rose. 'Are you by any chance acquainted with the Honourable Cedric Farley? I don't think you possibly can be, sir…He's a moonling!'

Once again his lordship was forced to exercise the firmest control in order to conceal his amusement. His daughter was nothing if not brutally candid. 'And what were your objections to both Pelham and Neubert, may I ask?'

'A pair of tailor's dummies!'

'God in heaven!' His lordship clapped a hand over his eyes. 'Where in the world do you learn such expressions?'

The exaggerated raising of one brow was a clear indication that she considered the question totally unnecessary. 'From the male members of this household, who else?'

Not best pleased at suddenly finding himself at a disadvantage, the Earl went striding back across to his desk. 'I'll have a word with that brother of yours when next I see him. He must learn to put a guard on his tongue when you're about.'

'I'm reliably informed that Marcus should be arriving any time now, and intends to stay in town for a week or two. I must say though, Papa, I think you're being grossly unfair to take him to task,' she pointed out in her absent half-brother's defence, 'especially as you yourself use the most appalling cant when in my presence.'

He was about to refute this, but then thought better of it and, instead, scooped up and waved the letters he had received during the past two weeks from those four hapless suitors. 'Don't think that you can lead me away from the matter in hand, you cunning little minx!'

The only effect this mild rebuke had on his headstrong daughter was to make her smile more brilliantly, and his lordship's annoyance finally got the better of him. 'You appear to take a light view of marriage, Sophia. Well, permit me to point out that it is a very serious business. An ill-judged choice of partner only brings misery to all concerned, and I do not intend that you should make a mistake in your choice of husband if it is within my power to prevent it. So, I have come to a decision.'

He paused for a moment to ensure that he had her full attention. 'I have made no secret of the fact that I intend to settle a large sum of money upon you when you marry. There is, however, a condition attached to my generosity. If you choose to marry without my consent, then your future husband had better possess sufficient funds to support you, because you will receive not a penny from me.' Again he paused while he tossed the letters from the rejected suitors back on the desk. 'Now, do I make myself clear?'

'Perfectly, sir. What you are trying to tell me is that I may marry whomsoever I choose providing he has wealth and belongs to our social class.' An ominous glint replaced the teasing sparkle in her eyes, as Sophia rose gracefully from the chair nearest to the hearth. 'It would appear, then, that I am destined to lead a life of hardship, for I would far rather be poor and married to a man of real worth than riveted to some empty-headed fribble whose only concern is how best to tie his cravat.'

His lordship could be as determined as his headstrong daughter when he chose, and refused to give way on this issue. 'I would suggest that you go up to your room and think very seriously about this matter,' he remarked, unbending.

Obediently she moved across to the door, but turned back to add, eyes still glinting, though whether in anger or devilment or a mixture of both, his lordship wasn't perfectly sure. 'Of course I shall do as you wish, but not for any great length of time. Mama would not be best pleased if I were late in putting in an appearance at my very own ball.' And with that quite deliberately provocative remark she left the room, and her father wondering what he had ever done that the gods should have seen fit to curse him with such a headstrong chit of a girl.

The Countess, emerging from the front parlour in

time to see her daughter mount the stairs, was not slow to notice the stubborn set of those lovely features, and knew even before she entered the library to find her husband glowering out of the window that the interview had not progressed quite as he might have wished.

'I assume Vale's offer received the same contemptuous refusal as the other three,' she remarked, seating herself in the chair recently vacated by Sophia.

'That daughter of yours is impossible!' his lordship snapped. Which, of course, was answer enough.

'Why is it, Thomas, that she is always my daughter whenever she has displeased you in some way, and your darling little Sophie at all other times?'

Annoyed though he was, he could not help smiling at this undeniable truth. He turned to look at the woman who had brought real peace and contentment to his life, and not for the first time blessed Providence for ensuring that their paths had crossed all those years ago out in India.

Unlike Danielle, his first wife, Marissa had never possessed any real claim to beauty, not even in her youth, and yet his lordship considered that her many wonderful qualities had withstood the test of time, whereas mere prettiness never could. She had proven to be a devoted wife and loving mother to their own offspring, and even though she had failed completely to cement a maternal bond with Marcus, the only child by his first marriage, his eldest son had never made any secret of the fact that he held his stepmother in the highest esteem.

A sigh escaped him as he drew his mind back to the present, and seated himself in the chair on the opposite side of the hearth. 'I fear, my dear, that I have made a mull of it all. Sophia flatly refuses even to consider Vale's offer.'

Her ladyship smiled faintly. 'Can you honestly say that you're surprised? He is, after all, a good deal older than she. Apart from his wealth, he has little to commend him, and I'm afraid the size of a gentleman's fortune would have very little influence on our daughter.'

'She has made that abundantly clear.' The Earl's grey brows snapped together, clearly revealing his continuing displeasure. 'Of course, all this flagrant disregard for wealth and rank was instilled in her at that confounded school. She ought never to have gone there, Marissa! That Guarding creature is nothing short of a revolutionary, with her nonsensical notions of equality.'

Once again the Countess smiled that serene smile of hers. 'If you recall, Thomas, we both agreed that Sophia would benefit from a year or two away at school. It was, let me remind you, you who insisted that she should not be placed in any one of those superior seminaries in Bath, where she would be absent from home for weeks at a time. The Guarding Academy, being situated so close to home, and having such a good reputation, was the most obvious choice.

And as regards what she learnt there…' Her ladyship reached for her embroidery and began calmly to ply her needle. 'She learnt nothing from Mrs Guarding that you yourself did not instil in all your children. From an early age all four of them were taught to treat those less fortunate than themselves with fairness and civility. And that, my dear Thomas, is precisely why we rarely have a servant wishing to leave our employ.'

He found himself quite unable to argue with this. 'Very true, my dear,' he concurred. 'I do believe in treating good and loyal servants courteously, but that doesn't mean I'd be content to have a footman as a son-in-law.'

Her ladyship's brows rose at this. 'And what on earth makes you suppose that there is any likelihood of that occurring?'

'Because that confounded daughter of yours can be quite stubbornly headstrong when the mood takes her!' his lordship retorted, irritation surfacing again. 'She as good as informed me that nothing would induce her to marry a member of her own social class, and that she would far rather be poor and riveted to some impoverished nobody, would you believe?'

The Countess regarded her husband in silence for a moment, realising suddenly that far more had taken place between father and daughter than she had at first realised. 'Why should Sophia imagine that she will ever be poor? She is an heiress. You have agreed to settle a fortune on her.'

For the first time his lordship betrayed clear signs of unease. 'Only on condition she marries with my full approval,' he mumbled, already regretting having issued such a threat.

It was only to be expected that a girl accustomed to having most everything her own way almost from the day of her birth would kick over the traces when finding herself harnessed for the very first time. But what choice had he? He had only her best interests at heart. Why in heaven's name couldn't the headstrong chit see that!

Feeling suddenly weary, he leaned back in his chair. 'Oh, Marissa, I'm at a loss to know what to do for the best. I'm one-and-seventy. I can't live for ever. I do not doubt for a moment that the boys will go on very well without me, but who will take care of my little Sophia when I'm gone?'

Refusing to become depressed at discussing such a melancholy topic, her ladyship said, 'Marcus will, I'm certain, admirably fill your shoes when the time comes. Which I sincerely trust will not be for several years yet.' She clearly heard the faint derisive snort. 'You do Marcus a grave injustice, my dear, if you suppose for a moment that he would neglect his responsibilities. He has looked after your estate in the north superbly during these past years. I know that he sometimes seems hard and unapproachable, but beneath that prickly exterior he is a very considerate man. He is very fond of his twin brothers, and of Sophia in particular.'

Much to his intense regret, his lordship had never been able to deal well with his eldest child. None the less, he was fair-minded enough to admit that his wife was right. 'But remember, my dear, that Marcus will one day marry himself, and raise a family. He will not then wish to be saddled with the added burden of keeping his eye on his frequently wayward half-sister.'

'She might be wilful on occasions, Thomas,' her ladyship responded, once again finding herself coming to Sophia's defence, 'but she's no fool. She may still harbour some girlish romantic notions, but I believe she will think long and hard before she ties herself to any man.'

The Earl remained unconvinced, but the Countess had more faith in their daughter's judgement. 'Leave it to me, my dear,' she said in her placid way. 'I'll have a talk with her.'

Final arrangements for the ball kept the Countess occupied for the remainder of the afternoon. Even if this had not been the case she would still have refrained from searching out her daughter and raising the topic of marriage, simply because it could only make the situation worse if Sophia felt that both her parents were intent on her making a superb match before the Season was over.

In fact, nothing could have been further from the truth. Although the Countess could well understand her husband's concern over their only daughter's future, and could appreciate, too, even though he had not admitted to it in so many words, that he was eager to keep fortune-hunters at bay, she saw no earthly reason why Sophia should not relax and enjoy her first Season in London. If she did happen to make the acquaintance of some personable gentleman with whom she could happily spend the rest of her life, all well and good; if not…well, there was always next year.

It was in this very understanding mood that the Countess entered her daughter's bedchamber in time to see the skilful young abigail positioning a spray of silk flowers in Sophia's beautifully arranged black locks. Unlike her occasionally volatile daughter, her ladyship always kept a tight hold on her emotions, but there was definitely a hint of pride in her grey eyes as she studied her daughter's faultless appearance.

'My dear, you look utterly charming,' she announced in her quiet way, while nodding dismissal to the maid.

Although Mother Nature had been undoubtedly generous, blessing her with lovely face and figure to match, Sophia was singularly lacking in conceit, as she proved now by glancing at her reflection with scant enthusiasm. 'This is a very pretty gown, Mama, and I do like it very well, but I would have preferred to have it made up in dark blue or red. Madame Félice said that, with my colouring, vibrant shades would suit me best.'

'And Madame Félice has earned herself something of a reputation for never being wrong, I know,' the Countess responded. 'Nonetheless, I'm still old-fashioned enough to believe that only pastel shades are suitable for young ladies. After you're married, of course, the wearing of richer colours will be perfectly in order.'

She caught her daughter's suddenly assessing look in the dressing-table mirror, and smiled. No, she mused, there was precious little wrong with Sophia's understanding. Nor did she suppose for a moment that her daughter would disgrace herself by eloping with some penniless nobody, providing, of course, pressure was not brought to bear which might induce her to commit such folly.

'No, my dear, I didn't come to your room with the intention of discussing the subject of marriage,' she assured her, knowing precisely what was going through that pretty little head. 'I should imagine you've heard more than enough on that particular topic for one day.'

Sophia almost sighed with relief. Her mother, always remarkably composed, was unfailingly sympathetic to the feelings of others. How she wished she could be more like her! Sadly, though, she feared she had inherited the occasionally fiery and frequently stubborn Cleeve temperament.

'I've never known Papa to be so unreasonable before. He seems to suppose that only a person of rank and wealth will make me a good husband.'

The Countess, appreciating only too well her poor husband's dilemma, remained silent. How could a loving father explain to a much beloved daughter that her hand might be sought in marriage for her fortune alone, without hurting her feelings?

'And yet it was he who instilled in us all,' Sophia went on, 'that a servant can exhibit just as much nobility as a duke. Perhaps he taught me too well, for I would much rather be married to a good and worthy man, no matter what his position on the social ladder, than marry a titled gentleman simply because by doing so I could continue to live in luxury.' She cast her mother a look of entreaty. 'You can understand that, can't you, Mama?'

'Better than you think, my dear. What you are trying to say is that you wish to marry a man you can love and respect and, moreover, a man who will love and respect you in return.' Seating herself on the *chaise-longue*, she held out her hand and waited for her daughter to join her before adding, 'Your father wants that too. He is only concerned for your happiness, Sophia. He would do everything within his power to ensure that you do not make the mistake that he once made.'

The Earl's first marriage was a subject that was rarely mentioned—taboo, almost. Sophia had, none the less, learned enough over the years from elderly servants and friends of the family to be certain that her father bitterly regretted marrying the beautiful Danielle.

'Yes, I do understand,' she said softly. 'But I have yet to meet a man with whom I could happily spend the rest of my life. I'm afraid, Mama, that the Lord Vales of this world are not to my taste.'

'Middle-aged dandies were never to mine either, child,' the Countess confessed, giving her daughter's hand an affectionate pat. 'There is no earthly reason why you should accept a proposal of marriage if you do not wish to. Sooner or later I feel certain that you will meet some personable young gentleman who will succeed in capturing your heart, but until such time, do not worry your pretty head over it any more.'

This was easier said than done. Although slightly reassured by her mother's understanding attitude, Sophia remained decidedly troubled. She hated being at odds with her father, while at the same time she continued to resent the unreasonable stand he had adopted. Was it her fault that four gentlemen had proposed marriage to her since her arrival in town? She certainly hadn't offered any one of them the least encouragement, unless agreeing to partner someone in a dance was considered sufficient inducement for a gentleman to propose marriage.

It was all so ridiculous, she decided, rising to her feet and accompanying her mother from the room. She had barely exchanged more than a dozen words with any one of those rejected suitors, so what on earth had made them suppose that she would make an ideal wife?

She was not so small-minded as to suppose that

just because love at first sight was a phenomenon that she herself had failed to experience the event never took place. She was well aware, too, that gentlemen were frequently beguiled by a pretty face. She could not help wondering, though, whether she would appear quite so appealing to certain members of the opposite sex if it were not for the fifty thousand pounds her father had promised to settle upon her when she married.

A slow and wickedly calculating smile curled the corners of what one besotted young fop had been overheard to call the most kissable mouth in London, as Sophia caught sight of her father standing at the entrance to the ballroom in readiness to greet the first of the guests. His threat to disinherit her if she married without his approval might well be turned to her advantage. If it became common knowledge that she wasn't an heiress at all, those offers for her hand might swiftly lessen and, with any luck, cease altogether, leaving her free to enjoy her first Season in London without causing further friction between her and her sire.

The idea, once firmly embedded, quickly began to grow, and Sophia had little difficulty in putting her plan into effect by dropping a word here and there into a receptive ear. Although the Season had not officially begun, London was certainly not thin of company, and invitations to the Yardley ball had been eagerly accepted. Among the four hundred guests were many hopeful mamas whose daughters sadly

possessed scant claim to beauty. It was only to be
expected, therefore, that some doting parents would
be only too willing to pass on unfavourable snippets
concerning a dangerous rival, especially if it increased
their own offspring's chances of achieving a suitable
match.

Consequently, as the evening progressed, Sophia
became increasingly satisfied with the many long and
thoughtful glances cast in her direction. She was not
so foolish as to suppose for a moment that everyone
would believe the rumour which was circulating
about her, nor did she consider that a supposed lack
of fortune would deter every gentleman from making
her an offer, and made allowances for this contin-
gency by not standing up with the same gentleman
more than once.

Nevertheless, she was never short of a partner, and
the evening was well advanced before she managed
to leave the dance floor and search out her good friend
Robina Perceval, who also happened to be enjoying
her first London Season.

'This is a truly magnificent ball,' Robina announced when Sophia had almost slumped, exhausted, in the vacant chair beside her. 'I do not think
I've ever seen so many people crowded into one room
before. The dances Aunt Eleanor organises at the
Angel back home are nothing to it.'

Sophia was not so impressed. Unlike Robina, who
lived a rather quiet life at the vicarage in Abbot
Quincey, a small market town situated within easy

walking distance of the Cleeves' country home, Sophia had attended many large parties since the age of sixteen. 'Yes, a dreadful squeeze, isn't it? You'll need to accustom yourself to such gatherings, Robin, because I'm reliably informed that a party isn't considered a success unless you're forever stepping on someone's toes.'

She took a moment to gaze about the crowded ballroom, trying to pick out the odd familiar face. 'I was sorry to learn that your cousin Hester would not be attending, but her brother Hugo is here. I danced with him earlier.'

'I understand that Aunt Eleanor and Hester will not be arriving in town until April.' Robina couldn't help but smile. 'I think if it was left to Hester she wouldn't be coming at all. Unlike Hugo, she has no taste for town life. She would much prefer to remain locked away in that attic room of hers. Though what she finds to keep her so occupied up there for hours at a time is anybody's guess. Who would believe a brother and sister could be so dissimilar!'

Her smile faded as she glanced at her friend's lovely profile. They had known each other most all their lives, and had always been the very best of friends, so Robina experienced no hesitation in saying, 'I think you should know that there is a rather unpleasant rumour circulating about you tonight.' It was then she noticed the betraying twitch at the corner of her friend's mouth. 'Never tell me that you put

it about that you haven't a feather to fly with! What
on earth possessed you?'

Well aware that the vicar's daughter would never
betray a confidence, Sophia didn't hesitate in enlight-
ening her. 'So you see,' she went on, after repeating
the gist of the interview with her father earlier in the
day, 'I was forced to do something to stem these ridiculous proposals of marriage. And it isn't as if the
rumour is a lie. Papa has threatened to disinherit me
if I marry against his wishes.' A defiant little gleam
sprang into her eyes. 'And to be perfectly honest with
you, at this precise moment in time I'm inclined to
do precisely that.'

Robina sat silently digesting what she had learned.
She had been taught to consider envy a sin, but
couldn't help feeling a touch resentful over her
friend's privileged position. Their circumstances were
vastly contrasting. Sophia could reject suitors at will,
whereas she herself would need to consider very carefully any offer of marriage that came her way. There
was no fault to find with her lineage: both her parents
came from noble stock. The Perceval name was an
old and honoured one, but that did not alter the fact
that she was little more than a country parson's
daughter whose dowry was woefully small. Her parents, though comfortably circumstanced, were by no
means wealthy, and they most certainly could not afford a second London Season for their eldest daughter
with three younger ones eagerly waiting to be
launched into society. So Robina felt it her duty to

accept any reasonable offer of marriage. But how she wished that she too could marry just for love!

'I have been away from the steadying influence of the vicarage a few days only,' she remarked with a wry little smile, 'yet already I'm in danger of being corrupted by the dangerously frivolous lures and heady atmosphere of the metropolis.'

Sophia frankly laughed. 'My staid little friend being led astray…? By whom or what, may I ask?'

'I shall explain some other time, for unless I much mistake the matter, a gentleman is approaching, with every intention of asking you to dance.'

Lord Nicholas Risely was, indeed, heading in their direction. Tall, slim and very good-looking, he was a firm favourite with a great many of society's leading hostesses and, consequently, was invited everywhere. His attire was faultless, his address excellent, and as he just happened to be the son of a duke, albeit a younger one, he was looked upon as being a very eligible *parti*.

In the normal course of events these facts alone would have prompted Sophia to add his name to that list of gentlemen best avoided, but she had not. Instead, she had permitted him to add his name to her dance card, simply because she had been most reliably informed that Lord Nicholas Risely was not on the look-out for a wife.

Happily allowing him to lead her onto the dance floor, she couldn't help noticing the strange look he cast her as they prepared to join one of the sets.

'Something appears to be troubling you, my lord,' she remarked. 'I cannot imagine you are concerned over making a cake of yourself. You are such an excellent dancer.'

As luck would have it the steps of the dance separated them, which granted Lord Nicholas the opportunity of formulating a response. Having met her on two occasions before, he had already decided that he rather liked Sophia Cleeve. She was bright and witty, nothing like the majority of simpering misses who flooded the marriage mart every year. If he had not been quite content to continue with his bachelor existence for a few years longer, she would have been just the sort of girl that would have appealed to him.

She was immensely pleasing on the eye, too. Perhaps not a beauty in the true classical style, but certainly lovely enough to prompt many a spiteful tabby with a daughter of her own to launch to start spreading malicious gossip about lack of fortune in the hope of making the lovely Lady Sophia appear far less desirable. It was all so unfair, so underhanded, and he for one had no intention of aiding any matchmaking mama's cause by repeating what he had overheard that night.

'Nothing troubling me at all, my lady,' he assured her, as they came together again. 'Couldn't be happier. This is a wonderful ball, and I am honoured to be dancing with its belle.'

'How very gallant of you to say so, Lord Nicholas! Had any other gentleman said such a thing I would have been instantly on my guard, but with you I know I'm perfectly safe.'

Now what the deuce did she mean by that? he wondered, as they separated, and didn't hesitate to ask for an explanation when they came together again.

'Simply that your good friend Freddy Fortescue assures me that you're not about to relinquish your bachelor status quite yet and, therefore, I can accept your compliments without fear that you will be foolish enough to follow them up with a proposal of marriage.'

Nicholas blinked. This was plain-speaking of the highest order, and he wasn't certain that he cared for it very much. He might not have any intention of asking this chit, or any other for that matter, to marry him, but it was very lowering to be told that one's suit would never be welcomed anyway.

Sophia was not slow to notice the flicker of annoyance. 'I've offended you, my lord, and I never meant to do so,' she assured him, her dazzling smile going some way to soothe a young gentleman's bruised ego. 'It's just that I too am in no hurry to relinquish my single state either, and when I do it will never be to a member of the Ton.'

He thought for a moment that she couldn't possibly be serious, that she might well be indulging in some wicked jest. Then he recalled being informed earlier in the evening that Lord Vale's suit had not prospered. The gentleman himself was not present tonight to confirm this or not, though whether his absence stemmed from pique at having been rejected, or having a prior engagement, was anyone's guess.

'You see, Lord Nicholas, men of wealth and rank hold no appeal for me.' Sophia decided that it could only aid her cause to spread this about. 'I am determined to marry a worthy man, no matter how lowly his station in life.'

'A footman, rather than a marquis; a groom rather than a duke,' he suggested, half-joking. 'I rather think your father will have a thing or two to say about that, Lady Sophia.'

'Oh, he already has, believe me,' she didn't hesitate to disclose, 'but his threat to disinherit me is certainly no deterrent.'

Still doubtful whether to believe her or not, he returned her to her pretty friend's side once the dance came to an end, and promptly moved away in order to sample some of the excellent refreshments being served that evening. He had only just relieved a footman of a glass of champagne when he received a tap on the shoulder, and heard an imperious voice enquire, 'Well, Risely, is what I've learned true or not?'

He turned to discover that most feared patroness of Almack's regarding him with haughtily raised brows. Had it been anyone else he might have been tempted not to answer, but one ignored Sally Jersey at one's peril. 'Couldn't say for certain, ma'am, one way or t'other. Shouldn't imagine so, though, would you? The Earl of Yardley seems dashed too fond of his daughter to disinherit her.'

She dismissed this with a wave of one slender hand. 'I'm not talking about that piece of utter nonsense. I really don't know how these foolish rumours get started. No, it was to Sharnbrook I was referring. I ran into your sister the other day, paying one of her rare visits to town, and she mentioned that nothing had been heard from your brother in months.'

'Oh, aye, that's right enough,' he confirmed, betraying what some might consider a callous lack of concern. 'We received a letter from him six months ago, after he had learned of our father's death, stating his intention of returning to this country before the end of the year. Can only imagine that something must have detained him out there in Jamaica.'

'Well, you may tell him from me, when he does return, that he's not to hide himself away in that magnificent ancestral home of his. We hostesses need him here in London. Such a matrimonial prize! Why, all the young ladies will be eager to capture his interest.'

'Oh, no—not quite all,' he murmured, catching sight of a raven-haired beauty being led once again on to the dance floor.

Chapter Two

Lord Nicholas Risely was among the first guests to leave the ball. He certainly managed to raise a few startled brows when he took his gracious leave of the host and hostess, for he had gained the reputation, since entering society two years before, of being a very sociable young man whose energy seemed boundless. Rarely did he seek the comfort of his bed much before three in the morning, once the social rounds had begun. Tonight, however, he seemed to have lost his desire for company, enjoyable though the Yardley ball had been.

Without waiting for a servant to find him a hackney carriage, he stepped outside into the cool night air and, heedless of any possible footpad lurking in this fashionable part of the town, walked briskly in the direction of his small but comfortable London home.

Although he had managed to appear sublimely un-concerned at the time, his short conversation with Lady Jersey had renewed those feelings of disquiet over his brother's safety which had plagued him increasingly during these past weeks. In the last letter sent from Jamaica, Benedict had clearly stated his intention of returning to the land of his birth some time during the autumn. That was almost six months ago, and nothing had been heard from him since.

It was quite possible, of course, that he had been forced to change his plans and had delayed his departure. It was equally possible that a letter informing his family of his revised plans had gone astray. Nevertheless Nicholas could not wholly dismiss the possibility, no matter how hard he tried, that some accident had befallen the Seventh Duke of Sharnbrook.

Long sea voyages were dangerous undertakings at the best of times, and more so during these past troubled years. Britain's splendid navy might be master of the seas, but those gallant sailors could not guard every stretch of water, and an attack from a French vessel was an ever-present danger. More disturbing still was the memory of those vicious gales which had wreaked havoc along the coast during the winter months, whipping the seas into a frenzy and causing more than one vessel to come to grief. The Atlantic was a vast ocean; any sailing ship foundering out there miles from land might not be reported missing for some considerable time.

He tried not to dwell on this dreadful possibility as he arrived back at his house. Not only had he a sincere regard for the brother he had not seen for more than half a decade, but he had no desire whatsoever to step into Benedict's shoes as head of the family. He was more than content with his carefree bachelor existence, and although he didn't consider himself to be in the least light-minded, he recoiled at the mere thought of having to accept responsibility for the running of the family's vast estate in Hampshire, not to mention the other sizeable properties dotted about the land.

Extracting the key from his pocket, he let himself inside the house. As he was never very sure of precisely when he would be returning home, he never encouraged his worthy factotum to wait up for him, and was faintly surprised to discover his butler-cum-valet dozing in the comfortable leather-bound chair in the hall.

'What's all this, Figgins? Why aren't you abed, man?' he demanded, as the servant awoke with a start at the closing of the door.

Having been in service most of his life, Figgins was quite accustomed to the ways of the nobility, and was not in the least offended by his young master's rather impatient tone.

Although he had always considered himself to be a very superior valet, he had not been averse, after his previous master had passed away, to accepting a position as general factotum in this small but fashionable household. He had worked for Lord Nicholas for the past two years, and could say with a clear conscience that not once had he ever committed the least solecism—never until tonight.

Rising to his feet, he cast a faintly concerned look in the direction of the parlour. 'I felt it my duty, sir, in the—er—circumstances, to await your return in order to apprise you.'

'Apprise me of what, may I ask?' Nicholas prompted when his very correct manservant cast a further glance in the direction of the parlour's closed door.

'Of the fact, sir, that there is someone else awaiting your return.'

Nicholas, having by this time divested himself of his outdoor garments, gave his servant his full attention. It was by no means unusual for him to return home in the early hours to discover one of his many friends sound asleep on the couch in the parlour, so he was at a loss to understand why Figgins should be making such an issue of the fact.

'Well, who is it? Harry Harmond?'

'No, sir. It is someone I've certainly never seen before.' Figgins, who rarely displayed the least emotion, permitted himself a thin smile of satisfaction. 'I have always prided myself on being an excellent judge of character, able to pinpoint very accurately a person's station in life. And I certainly know an encroaching individual when I see one.' His smile disappeared. 'But I am forced to admit that the person who called shortly after you had left the house, and who is now comfortably ensconced in the parlour, has me well and truly puzzled. His appearance leaves—er—much to be desired, as you might say, but his speech and manners are those of an undoubted gentleman. I have therefore formed the opinion, sir, although he stubbornly refused to give his name, that he must be an old acquaintance of yours who has, perhaps, fallen on hard times.'

For a few moments it was as much as Nicholas could do to gape in open-mouthed astonishment. 'And you let him in? Good gad, man, you must be all about in your head!'

Nicholas was by no means a hard-hearted person, and would willingly come to the aid of a friend, should the need arise, but he refused to be taken advantage of by some rascally individual he barely knew. 'What in the world prompted you to admit him? The rogue has probably taken himself off long since. And with all my best silver, if I know anything!'

'Oh no, sir. He hasn't done that,' Figgins responded, completely unruffled. 'And I can assure you, sir, that I would never have permitted him to set foot inside the house, let alone provide him with supper and a glass or two of wine, if it hadn't been for the fact that he informed me that he had news concerning your brother.'

'Oh, he has, has he?' Nicholas was decidedly sceptical. 'Well, his tidings had better be worth the food and drink he's consumed already at my expense,' he ground out, throwing wide the parlour door, and striding purposefully into the room to discover the shabbily dressed individual sprawled at his ease in the most comfortable chair in the house. 'Otherwise he'll find himself helped on his way by the toe of my boot!'

A slow and lazy smile tugged at the corners of the visitor's well-shaped mouth, but the eyes remained firmly closed as he said, 'I shall take leave to inform you that I consider that a most impolite greeting to offer someone you haven't seen for several years, dear brother.'

Nicholas stopped dead in his tracks, once again powerless to prevent his jaw from dropping perceptively when the lids of dazzling blue eyes finally opened and the visitor rose to his feet in one graceful movement. 'Benedict?' he murmured, taking a hesitant step forward. Then, 'Ben, by all that's wonderful!...It is you!'

Figgins, hovering in the open doorway, experienced a sense of pride as he watched the two men clasp each other warmly. It was comforting to know that his instincts had not played him false and that the very welcome visitor, taller than his brother by an inch or two, and noticeably broader, had turned out to be what he had suspected from the start—a gentleman of quality.

He coughed delicately, thereby indicating his continued presence, and the brothers loosened their hold. 'Do you wish me to fetch brandy, m'lord?'

'Yes. Yes, of course,' Nicholas answered, still

somewhat bemused by his sibling's unexpected arrival. 'And make sure it's the best brandy, Figgins. This calls for a celebration.'

After his servant had departed, Nicholas busied himself for a minute or two by going about the room lighting more candles, and then joined his brother by the hearth. He was quite unable to forbear a smile as he watched Benedict piling more logs on what was already a substantial fire. Evidently the British climate no longer agreed with him, which was hardly surprising after spending so many years abroad. This, however, was by no means the most obvious change in him.

No one viewing him now would ever have supposed for a moment that Benedict had once been considered a dandy, rivalling the famous Beau Brummell himself in dress. Nicholas recalled quite clearly watching his brother on numerous occasions, sitting before a dressing-table mirror, patiently tying intricate folds in a highly starched cravat until he had it just so. Yet here he sat, now, with a gaudy red kerchief tied about his throat, his long legs encased in a pair of rough homespun trousers, and a slightly soiled and heavily creased shirt encasing that broad expanse of chest. Why, he looked little better than a vagrant with that mass of golden-brown hair almost touching his shoulders. And the weeks of growth on and around his chin did absolutely nothing to improve his appearance!

'By that disapproving look,' Benedict remarked, after raising his striking blue eyes in time to catch his brother's frowning scrutiny, 'I assume my appearance does not meet with your approval.'

'Good gad, Ben! You resemble nothing so much as a rascally vagrant.'

'I am relieved the hard-working soul who gave me these clothes isn't present,' Benedict responded, with more than a hint of wryness. 'He would have been most offended. This shirt, I am assured, was his very best. Though it isn't strictly true, I suppose, to say that he gave me these clothes,' he corrected. 'We struck a bargain. I exchanged them for a suit of my own. And was heartily glad to do so! I was sick and tired of my own apparel after several weeks at sea.'

'Do you mean to say you exchanged all your clothes for those…those deplorable rags?' Nicholas did not believe a word of it. 'You must take me for a half-wit if you think I'll swallow that one.'

'True as I sit here, dear brother,' Benedict assured him. 'Except I only gave him the clothes I stood up in. They were all I had, you see. Pirates deprived me of the rest.'

Once again Nicholas found himself gaping. 'Pirates? What pirates?'

'The ones we unfortunately encountered two days after setting sail from Port Royal.' Benedict smiled at his young brother's decidedly sceptical look. 'Sailing through the Caribbean is not the same as taking a boat trip down the Thames, dear boy. It is still a dangerous place. Many people of varying nationalities, fleeing from the law, seek refuge there. Piracy is still quite common, believe me.'

'What happened?' Nicholas prompted, suddenly resembling an excited schoolboy, and Benedict was of a mind to be indulgent.

'The captain of our ship, being a Christian soul, could not find it within himself to blithely ignore what appeared to be a vessel in distress, and gave the order to heave-to. Grappling-hooks were thrown with remarkable speed, and before the captain and crew realised what was happening we were being boarded by a horde of cut-throats. The captain and crew of our ship gave a good account of themselves, as did a couple of the passengers, and we soon had the rogues returning to their own vessel, but not before they had deprived us of some of the food on board, and several other items of worth, including my trunk, which contained not only my clothes, but my valuables, too. Consequently all I was left with were the clothes I stood up in. And, as you can imagine, by the time we had docked in Liverpool, I was heartily glad to be rid of them, even to exchange them for the ones I'm wearing now.'

Nicholas could well understand this and smiled, until a thought suddenly occurred to him. 'How on earth did you manage to reach London without money? Surely you didn't walk?'

'Thankfully, I wasn't reduced to that, though it could hardly have been more uncomfortable than travelling by the common stage. I have grown accustomed to doing without many creature comforts during my time in Jamaica, but sitting for hours in a vehicle that smells of perspiration, onions, and various other unpleasant odours was almost more than I could bear.'

His pained expression almost had his young brother writhing in laughter. 'No, I still retained my pocket watch, which I was able to sell for half its real value. I swear the rogue who purchased it in Liverpool thought it had been stolen.'

'I can't say I'm surprised,' Nicholas responded when he had gained sufficient control of himself. 'No one would take you for a member of the peerage!'

'That isn't strictly true,' Ben corrected. 'Your estimable butler, unless I much mistake the matter, managed to penetrate the disguise.' He glanced round as the door opened, his face brightening. 'And here he is, and armed, I see, with more of that delicious apple tart.'

'I thought, perhaps, you could manage another mouthful, your grace,' Figgins said, placing the tray containing the food and brandy down on a convenient table near his master's chair. 'Will there be anything else you require, sir?'

'Yes, you'd best make the bed up in the spare room, and look out one of my night-shirts.' Nicholas turned his attention back to his brother as soon as Figgins had left the room. 'There's only a skeleton staff now at the house in Grosvenor Square. The place hasn't been used since Father died.'

He searched in vain for a sign of remorse on his brother's handsome face, and yet he knew how fond Benedict had been of their father. 'He passed away peacefully in his sleep. He didn't suffer,' he assured him, and this time Benedict responded with a softly spoken, 'I'm glad,' and then promptly changed the subject by enquiring after their sister.

'Oh, Connie's in fine fettle. Put on some weight since the last time you saw her. Still,' he shrugged, 'only to be expected at her age. Increased the progeny by three since you've been away. Five of the little blighters she's produced now. Which says something for Lansdown, I suppose. I have a deal of respect for our dear brother-in-law. Poor chap must possess the patience of a saint to put up with our bird-witted sister.'

Benedict, willingly accepting a further slice of the apple tart and a full measure of the brandy, could not suppress a smile. No doubt Constance continued to treat Nicholas as though he were still a mischievous schoolboy, and his evident resentment was quite understandable. He decided to make his own feelings known.

'I perceive a great change in you, Nick.' He took a moment to study the very fashionable attire. 'Apeing the dandy yourself now, I see.'

'One must dress, dear brother.' The pained expression returned as his attention was drawn to that gaudy neck decoration once more. 'Just as well you did come straight here. Wouldn't do to let people see you

looking like that, you know. There's the name to consider, and all that,' he remarked with quaint snobbery.
'We'll rise early tomorrow and pay a visit to a tailor…Or perhaps several.'

The following morning Benedict discovered that
his brother's idea of rising early was not quite the
same as his own. So, after he had consumed a hearty
breakfast of ham, eggs and buttered rolls, washed
down with several cups of freshly-brewed coffee, and
there were still no signs that Nicholas was ready to
leave the comfort of his bedchamber and face the new
day, Benedict decided to pass the time by exploring
the metropolis to see what changes had taken place
during his years away.

He stepped outside to discover a morning that was
both dry and bright, and blessedly free from the evil
choking fog that often shrouded the city even at this
time of year. His athletic, long-striding gait quickly
brought him to the end of the street and into a wider
thoroughfare, where hordes of people were now busily going about their daily work.

This was the part of the city that he knew best of
all, where pretty girls in white pinafores and black
taffeta bonnets were parading the fashionable streets
and squares dispensing milk from the buckets they
carried, their cries mingling with those of other hawk-
ers, eager to sell their wares. This was where he had
happily frittered away his time, and money, paying
visits to friends and enjoying the many pleasurable

activities the capital had to offer any young gentleman of wealth and rank. This was what, five years ago, he had very much resented being forced to leave behind.

He remembered clearly the bitterness he had felt when his father had insisted that he travel to Jamaica and learn to respect the value of money by taking charge of the family's plantation out there. Their parting had been an unpleasant one, with many biting recriminations uttered on both sides. Not many months had passed, however, before Benedict had come to realise that his father's actions had been totally justified, and he could only be thankful that the majority of letters exchanged during their years apart had been full of warmth and understanding; his only real regret now being that he had not returned to England in time to see his father one last time before his death.

Yes, those years in Jamaica had changed him completely. He was no longer that care-for-nobody, that frivolous, pleasure-seeking fribble whose only ambition was to cut a dash in society, and who squandered vast sums of money without a thought to whose hard work financed his pleasures or from whence the money had come. Older and, hopefully, wiser now, he believed he could take his father's place and carry out his duties as head of the family in a responsible and caring manner. The cut of a jacket, the set of a cravat and a looking-glass shine on a pair of boots were no longer important to him. A sigh escaped him. Nevertheless he supposed it behoved him to take his brother's advice, and attire himself as befitted his station in life before returning to the fashionable world, a world that, if the truth were known, he had little desire to re-enter.

The stink of rotting refuse and equally unpleasant odours suddenly assailing his nostrils induced him to take stock of his surroundings. Without being aware of it, he had walked ever eastwards into those areas of the capital where most people of his class rarely or never ventured. The distinction between rich and poor could not have been more marked. There were no fine mansions here, no crossing-boys to clear away the filth from the streets, and no ladies and gentlemen, dressed in their finery, taking the air. Which was hardly surprising, he decided, ripping the kerchief from his neck and putting it to good use by placing it over his nose and mouth.

The air was foul, polluted by filth and grime which oozed from the tightly-packed hovels, and half-starved children, dressed in rags, or nothing at all, were grubbing round in the dirt. What it must be like here when the weather became warmer he dreaded to think. Little wonder these areas of the city harboured the constant threat of typhus. To the poor wretches living here disease and starvation were commonplace, a way of life from which there was little hope of escape.

He knew, of course, that it was the height of folly to remain in these noisome streets, where vice and corruption abounded on every corner, and yet he found his interest well and truly captured. So engrossed did he become in the heart-rending wretchedness surrounding him that it was not until almost noon that he ventured back to the more affluent part of the city, and was greeted none too politely when he did eventually return to his brother's house.

'Where the deuce have you been?' Nicholas demanded to know. 'Figgins informed me that you left the house hours ago.'

'That is correct.' Benedict joined him at the table, and helped himself to a cup of fresh coffee. 'I decided to occupy my time while waiting for you to rise in exploring the capital.'

'Expect you discovered some changes, eh?'

'Can't say I took much notice of the area round here. Whitechapel, Bethnal Green, Shoreditch and Smithfield certainly proved most interesting, though.'

'Good gad, Benedict!' Nicholas was beginning to wonder whether those years spent under a tropical sun might not have had some adverse effect on his brother's mental state. 'What on earth possessed you to venture to those spots? They're all notorious havens for every form of low life. Even the Runners won't enter those places alone, not even in broad daylight.' A disturbing possibility suddenly occurred to him. 'Dear Lord! You didn't go there to find a woman, did you?'

One ducal brow arched. 'Credit me with some intelligence. Not that I didn't receive several offers, but I have far too much respect for my health.'

'Well, thank the Lord for that!' his graceless brother responded, audibly sighing with relief. 'Though I'm rather surprised you managed to return totally unscathed.'

'Dressed as I am, I no doubt appeared one of their own and, therefore, not worthy of accosting.'

This candid response returned Nicholas's thoughts to what for him was the most pressing problem besetting him at the moment and, after hurriedly finishing his meagre repast, he wasted no further time in taking the first steps in putting his brother's deplorable appearance to rights.

It rather amused him to see the appalled expressions on those famous Bond Street tailors' faces when his brother entered their superior establishments in his wake. Benedict did not appear to take offence at the unenthusiastic reception he received wherever he went, and certainly displayed praiseworthy self-control when he was pulled this way and that, and measured with ruthless efficiency. Nicholas soon discovered, however, that beneath that veneer of complacency was an iron strong will, for nothing would induce Benedict to have his coats made fashionably tight, nor tempt him to select anything other than the plainest of colours for his clothes.

'Damned unimaginative! That's what I call it,' Nicholas remonstrated, as they emerged into the sunlight once more. 'Yellow-and-black-striped waistcoats are all the fashion this Season.'

'I do not doubt you are correct, brother. But I have

no intention of going about the capital resembling something that spends most of its life collecting pollen.'

Nicholas was about to cast further aspersions on what he considered a deplorably unimaginative taste, when he caught sight of one of his degenerate friends on the opposite side of the street, and took evasive action by concealing himself in a doorway.

'I have no intention either of wearing coats so close-fitting that one cannot breathe, or breeches so tight that they're in danger of splitting every time one sits down,' Benedict announced before he realised he was conversing with fresh air and, glancing round in an attempt to locate his sibling's whereabouts, promptly collided with something soft, slender and totally feminine emerging from Hookham's Library.

Benedict was powerless to prevent several books cascading from slender hands and ending up on the pavement, but managed to prevent the lady herself suffering the same fate by reaching out a steadying arm to encircle a very trim waist. 'I'm so very sorry,' he apologised, silently cursing his clumsiness, and was about to relinquish his hold when the head beneath the fashionable bonnet was suddenly raised.

For several moments it was as much as Benedict could do to stop himself gaping like some lovelorn fool as thickly lashed eyes, with a spark of mischief in their beautiful green depths, twinkled up at him, and perfectly moulded lips curled into the sweetest of smiles. Beauties he'd known by the score, but never before had the sight of a lovely face and trim figure held him so totally captive, mind and body under some hypnotic spell, quite unable to function. The sights and sounds around him slowly began to fade, and he was conscious only of her, and the ever-increasing desire never to relinquish his hold.

Nicholas, on the other hand, stepping out from the convenient hiding-place, was instantly aware of the interest his clumsy brother was arousing in several passers-by, and promptly took command of the situation by treading none too gently on one roughly shod foot. 'Don't just stand there like a dolt!' he ordered, sublimely ignoring the flashing look of annoyance he perceived in a pair of masculine eyes. 'Help this lady's maid to pick up those books!'

Very reluctantly Benedict did as bidden, and Nicholas wasted no time in escorting the young lady in question to her waiting carriage. 'Can't apologise enough. The clumsy brute might have done you a serious mischief. I trust you're none the worse for the encounter?'

'No, not at all, sir,' she assured him, her gaze momentarily wandering in the tall man's direction as he handed her maid the books. 'And please do not blame your servant. It was as much my fault as his. I was not attending where I was going either.'

Out of the corner of his eye Nicholas saw Benedict approaching, and hurriedly helped the lovely damsel into the carriage. 'You are too kind, ma'am,' he responded, stepping to one side to enable the maid to enter, and then wasted no time in closing the door.

'Why in heaven's name didn't you introduce me?' Benedict demanded, aggrieved, as he watched the carriage move away.

'What!' Once again Nicholas very much feared those years spent beneath a Caribbean sun had taken their toll. 'When I've done everything humanly possible to keep your identity secret since we left the house? You might have no pride in the name you bear, brother, but I most certainly have. Do you imagine I'll permit London to see you going about looking like that? Why, it would be the talk of the clubs for months to come if your identity ever became known!'

Catching the eye of a passing jarvey, Nicholas hurriedly bundled his troublesome brother into the hired carriage before Benedict could draw more attention to himself. 'I don't understand what's come over you, Ben. You used to take such pride in your appearance, and yet now you don't seem to care a whit that you look more like a didicoi than a duke.'

More interested in the lovely image his mind's eye was conjuring up, Benedict had listened with only half an ear to his brother's strictures. 'Who was she? Do you know?'

Nicholas cast him an impatient glance, wondering anew what had come over him. No one would have believed his brother capable of fending off an attack from pirates, when a pair of green eyes could fell him with one glance!

'Of course I know her. I was dancing with her only last night. She's Lady Sophia Cleeve, the Earl of Yardley's daughter.' He raised his eyes heavenwards when his brother's besotted expression did not alter. 'Anyone would suppose you'd never seen a pretty face before.'

'Pretty? A totally inappropriate description!' Benedict scoffed. 'She's exquisite.'

Nicholas considered this for a moment or two. 'Opinions differ. Some consider her a beauty. However, blondes are all the fashion this Season.'

His brother appeared decidedly unimpressed. Evidently flaxen hair was not to his taste. 'My, my, the little minx appears to have you well and truly in her toils,' Nicholas remarked, highly amused now by the unfortunate encounter with the Earl's daughter. 'Not that I don't think it's high time you were leg-shackled, brother, but if you take my advice you'll look elsewhere for a wife.'

A heart-rending possibility occurred to Benedict. 'She isn't married already, is she? Or engaged?'

'No, nor likely to be, either.'

'Why? What do you mean?'

'She doesn't seem interested in marriage. At least,' Nicholas amended, memory stirring, 'certainly not a marriage to a member of our class. If what she tells me is true, she prefers the company of grooms to dukes.'

'Ha! She must have been teasing you,' Benedict scoffed, thinking his brother highly gullible.

'Perhaps,' Nicholas conceded. 'I'm only repeating what I was told last night. Furthermore, she's received four proposals of marriage to my certain knowledge since her arrival in town, and has refused them all. Which would suggest that she certainly isn't hankering after a husband, let alone a title.' His wicked sense of humour coming to the fore, he gave a shout of laughter. 'Why, she paid more attention to you out there in the street just now than she pays to most members of her own class.'

Evidently his brother did not share the joke, for he sat silently staring out of the window. 'Don't disturb yourself,' Nicholas advised. 'There'll be plenty of other pretty wenches gracing the Season once it officially gets under way.'

'I dare say you're right,' Benedict murmured, a decidedly calculating gleam springing into his striking blue eyes, 'but it's Lady Sophia Cleeve I intend to get to know. So perhaps, all things considered, it might serve me best if I remain incognito for a while longer.'

'How on earth can that benefit you?' Nicholas asked, totally at a loss.

Benedict transferred his gaze to his sibling's puzzled countenance. 'You said yourself that she prefers the company of grooms…And if there is one thing I do know…it's my way around a stable!'

Chapter Three

The Earl of Yardley was essentially a man of habit, and his sojourn in the capital had not altered his routine to any great extent. Consequently, Cardew knew precisely where his master was to be found at this time of day, and entered the library to discover his lordship, as expected, seated at his desk, carefully studying his correspondence.

'I regret having to disturb you, sir,' he said, as the Earl, pausing in the perusal of the letter in his hand, raised an enquiring brow, 'but the head groom is here, requesting an interview with you.'

Like all the other servants, Cardew held his master in high esteem. During the twenty years he had been employed as butler in the Cleeve household he could never recall even one occasion when the Earl had been too busy to spare one of his employees some of his time, and he knew what the response would be even before his lordship said, 'Of course. I shall see him at once.'

Certain that his most loyal henchman would not seek an interview on some trivial matter, the Earl set aside his correspondence and a moment later watched his head groom enter, cap in hand, looking totally ill-at-ease, just as he always did whenever in elegant surroundings. Trapp was never happy when away from the stables for any length of time. Horses were his life, and his lordship suspected that he much preferred their company to that of most people.

'Well, come in, Trapp,' his lordship ordered when the groom, who had been with him all those years ago out in India, continued to hover by the door. 'What can I do for you?'

'I'm here on young Clem's behalf, sir.' Looking and sounding nothing like the iron-handed ruler of the stables whose word was law, and whose barking commands kept the youngest stable-lads in a permanent state of terror, he moved hesitantly across to the desk.

'Seemingly Clem's been offered a post as head groom on some large estate in the south, sir. I 'ave to say I don't want to lose 'im. He's a good lad and he's been with us for a number of years, but there's no denying it would be a good move for 'im.' His weather-beaten face creased into a semblance of a smile. 'I ain't quite ready to hang up the harness yet, as yer might say, so I can't blame Clem for not wanting to wait around until I do.'

His lordship nodded his head in agreement. 'Do you know precisely who has made him this offer of employment, Trapp?'

'That I don't, sir. Don't know that Clem does neither, if it comes to that. Or if he does, he ain't saying. Seemingly someone approached 'im when he were in The Red Lion t'other evening. Said that if he wanted the position, he'd 'ave to take it right away. He's been given until this evening to make up 'is mind.'

The Earl's silver-grey brows snapped together, clearly betraying his staunch disapproval. He considered this underhanded way of acquiring employees totally unacceptable. Why, it smacked of nothing short of poaching! Yet, at the same time, he could quite understand Clem's wishing to improve his lot, and felt it would be very mean-spirited on his part not to let the young groom go simply because he and Trapp would be put to the trouble of finding a suitable replacement.

'If Clem wishes to leave us, then we must accept the situation with a good grace,' he responded at length, echoing his thoughts aloud. 'It's unlikely we'll find a replacement at a moment's notice, so I'll arrange for one of the lads at Jaffrey House to come here.'

'There may be no need to put yourself to the bother, sir,' Trapp surprised his lordship by announcing. 'As luck would 'ave it, someone wandered into the mews this morning in search of work. Seemingly, he's been away in foreign parts for a number of years. Brown as a nut he be, so I don't doubt the truth o' that. Came back after his old master died, he told me.'

His lordship was not enthusiastic. 'Who was his

late employer, do you know? Can he supply a reference?'

'No, sir. Happen there were a spot o' bother on the
boat journey home. Lost all his belongings, so he told
me.'

'Mmm.' His lordship's brows once again met at the
bridge of his thin, aristocratic nose. 'You know my
views, Trapp. I'm never altogether happy about em-
ploying people who cannot provide a reference, especially strangers.'

'Aye, sir. I do know.' Trapp raised a hand to
scratch his grizzled hair: a habit of his when pondering a ticklish problem. 'And, ordinarily, I'm of a similar mind. But I 'ave to say that this fellow knows a
thing or two about beasts. It just so 'appens that Miss
Sophie's filly was in one of her frisky moods when
he wanders into the mews. Had her quietened down
in a trice, so he did. Beasts, I reckon, 'ave a deal more
sense than most folks. And what I always says is, if
horses take to a cove, then he can't be all bad.'

There was perhaps more than a grain of truth in
this simple philosophy, his lordship decided, and he
took a moment or two more to consider the matter.
'Very well, Trapp. If you're willing to give this
stranger a chance, that's good enough for me. If he
doesn't prove suitable, I can, as I've already mentioned, send to Jaffrey House for a replacement.'

Although he had given his consent readily enough,
his lordship was not completely happy with this unexpected turn of events. Was it mere coincidence, he

wondered, watching his henchman leave the room, that soon after his groom had been offered a new position, someone should have turned up looking for work? A wry smile tugged at the corner of his thin-lipped mouth. Perhaps he was just getting too cynical in his old age, he decided, his mind returning to something else which had puzzled him during the past few days.

Why, he wondered, had there been a marked lack of interest of late shown by eligible young gentlemen in his daughter? Since the night of their ball he had not received one offer, verbal or otherwise, for Sophia's hand. He was not so foolish as to suppose that he would be likely to receive a proposal of marriage every single week for the duration of their stay in town. Nor was he such a doting father that he imagined for a moment that his daughter, lovely though she was, would be to every man's taste.

There was no denying, either, that Sophia could be troublesome on occasions, and any gentleman hoping for a quiet life would do well to consider long and hard before proposing matrimony to her. Only a gentleman with a stronger will than her own could ever hope to keep Sophia under control. Surely, though, somewhere in the length and breadth of this land existed a gentleman of good birth quite capable of keeping a tight rein on a troublesome filly? His lordship could only hope that this was so, and that it wouldn't be too long before this ideal mate crossed his daughter's path.

The door opened and the subject of his thoughts, looking perfectly charming in a lavender silk gown and matching bonnet, swept into the room. The sweetly angelic smile on her face, as she tripped lightly across to the desk, would fool most gentlemen into believing that by nature she was compliant. A grossly inaccurate supposition which any poor deluded fool might make, he decided, his suspicions surfacing anew.

'What on earth have I done to make you scowl so, Papa?' After placing a kiss on the soft, silver-grey hair, she perched herself, uninvited, on the edge of his desk. 'Anyone seeing that disapproving look of yours might suppose that I'd been up to some mischief.'

'It is not beyond the realms of possibility that you have been, my dear,' he responded drily, thereby igniting that gurgle of feminine laughter which never failed to bring a smile to his own lips. 'Where are you off to this morning, decked out in all your finery?'

'I'm going out with Mama in the carriage to visit Madame Félice. I'm due there in an hour for the final fitting of my new riding habit, and we mustn't be late, otherwise we might find ourselves having to return some other time.'

'My, my! How things have changed!' his lordship remarked, in the same dry tone. 'In my day no seamstress would dare to dictate what time a member of the aristocracy was to arrive at her shop.'

'Ah! But she's no ordinary dressmaker, Papa. Anyone who is anyone has a gown made by Madame Félice,' Sophia remarked, wickedly mimicking the élite hostess whose ball she had attended the previous night. 'Ordinarily, as you know, that wouldn't weigh with me, but I am desperate to have my new habit finished. I haven't ridden once since we arrived in town.'

This innocent admission jogged his lordship's memory, and he wasn't in the least surprised by Sophia's crestfallen expression when he apprised her of Clem's wishing to leave, and the reason behind the young groom's decision.

'I shall be very sorry to see him go, Papa. I always preferred Clem to accompany me whenever I went out riding.' Slipping lightly from the desk, she went over to the door, but turned back as a dreadful thought suddenly occurred to her. 'That doesn't mean I shall be forced to take Trapp with me for the duration of our stay in town, does it? I shan't be able to do a thing without his reporting my comings and goings straight back to you.'

'And wouldn't that be a good thing!' his lordship retorted, wickedly teasing, and then laughed outright as Sophia gave a haughty toss of her head before sweeping regally from the room.

No, it certainly would be no bad thing for someone to keep an eye on the little monkey, he reiterated, silently revising his own plans for the forthcoming weeks.

Although he enjoyed good health, he was no longer a young man, and had decided long before they had embarked on this visit to the metropolis that he would be leaving the supervision of his most trying offspring in his wife's very capable hands. He had adjusted reasonably well already to town hours, but was very well aware that he no longer possessed the stamina, or the inclination for that matter, to throw himself headlong into the social whirl. None the less, it would not do him a mite of harm, he decided, if just every once in a while he accompanied his wife and daughter out for an evening. His added presence would certainly ensure his daughter's good behaviour. Furthermore, it would not hurt to have a word with Trapp, just to ensure that this new man was well aware that he must keep a strict watch whenever he accompanied the daughter of the house out on what might very well turn out to be a daily ride, if the weather continued fair.

Although Sophia had said very little when she had learned of Clem's wishing to leave, she was very up-set by the unexpected news. Clem had been her personal groom for more than ten years. Unfailingly vigilant, while at the same time allowing her free rein, he had proved to be the perfect bodyguard and companion during those innumerable rides they had taken across the Earl's Northamptonshire acres. Some would consider, she didn't doubt, that her manner towards the young groom had been far too free and easy, but Sophia had looked upon Clem more as a friend than a servant, and she felt that he would be very difficult to replace.

Consequently, when she entered the famous *modiste*'s premises in Bond Street, her mood was quite naturally subdued. Her mind locked in the past, recalling those numerous occasions when she and her trusty companion had explored far-afield areas of the Northamptonshire countryside, she hardly noticed the other customers sitting in the plush velvet chairs, nor did she realise that none other than the much coveted dressmaker herself had accompanied her into the fitting-room until a sweetly accented voice remarked, 'Your new habit does not please you, *mademoiselle*? Or is it, perhaps, something else that makes you unhappy this day?'

Drawing her mind back to the present, Sophia received something of a shock when she discovered the *modiste* studying her intently, the lovely blue eyes openly assessing. 'Oh, no, Madame, the habit is perfect.'

'Not quite,' the modiste countered, her professional eye quickly perceiving a slight fault. 'A little adjustment to the skirt is required. I hope then that you will look a little happier when you are wearing it, *petite*, otherwise my reputation *par excellence* will tumble, no?'

So the famous *modiste* had a sense of humour, had she? Sophia mused, quickly detecting the mischievous twinkle in the blue eyes. The dressmaker was possibly more amused than gratified by her meteoric rise to fame, and Sophia felt suddenly drawn to the woman who, she suspected, was not so many years older than herself.

'I assure you, madame, that the habit pleases me very much,' she assured her, taking care not to step on the soft velvet folds as she stepped out of the skirt. 'It is just that this morning I received some rather sad news. Someone who has worked for my family for many years is to leave us.'

The smile that curled the dressmaker's full lips appeared full of warmth and understanding. 'I think, perhaps, that the one that leaves you is something more than just a servant, *hein*?'

Sophia nodded. 'More a friend.'

'Then could you not, perhaps, persuade him to stay?' Madame suggested, helping Sophia to don the walking dress and matching pelisse which she herself had made for the Earl's daughter only the week before.

'I dare say I could, but I shan't make the attempt.' She caught the dressmaker's look of surprise in the large, oval mirror. 'He has been my personal groom for many years and, I believe, has been happy in his work, but now wishes to better himself. He has been offered the position of head groom on some country estate, though I know not which.' She moved one of her slender hands in a slight gesture of resignation. 'It would be selfish of me to try to stop him improving himself.'

The look that sprang into the *modiste*'s eyes was difficult to interpret, but Sophia thought she could detect a hint of respect in those striking blue depths.

'I do not think, *petite*, that you will have the least difficulty in finding a replacement,' the young dressmaker responded softly, as she held back the curtain for Sophia to pass into the elegant waiting-room.

'My, my, Sophia! You have been honoured this day,' her mother teased, after they had left the shop and had settled themselves in the carriage once more for the short journey back to Berkeley Square. 'Lady Strattan went quite pea-green with envy when Madame Félice selected to offer you her undivided attention. How does it make you feel to have eclipsed such a leading society hostess as the Marchioness of Strattan? The poor woman will never be able to hold her head up in public again!'

'You know full well, Mama, that I consider such things totally unimportant,' Sophia responded, chuckling at her mother's rather wicked sense of humour. 'I would have been just as content to have had one of the assistants attend to me, though I must confess, I did find the celebrated *modiste* most interesting,' she admitted, settling herself more comfortably on the seat. 'She isn't nearly so old as I had imagined. She's not many years older than myself, I shouldn't have thought. And she's extremely pretty too, though she does her level best to conceal the fact by wearing very plain gowns, and hiding her hair beneath a cap.'

'Perhaps she's still in mourning, dear,' her ladyship

suggested, memory stirring. 'I believe someone did mention that she's a widow.'

'Perhaps she is,' Sophia conceded, but remained doubtful. 'It wouldn't surprise me, though, if she had never been married at all. She wouldn't be the first female to feign the status of a married woman. Our very own housekeeper does precisely that.'

'Very true,' her ladyship concurred. 'I should imagine high-ranking female servants feel that adopting the status of a married woman adds to their respectability.'

'Just as dressmakers believe that pretending to be French will ensure their success.'

'Are you implying that you suspect Madame Félice is not a Frenchwoman, dear?'

Turning her head a little to one side, Sophia considered this. 'I'm not certain. That pretty accent of hers sounds genuine enough.'

'Well, you were certainly granted ample opportunity to form an opinion. You were in the fitting-room quite some considerable time,' her ladyship remarked. 'I trust there are not too many alterations needing to be made to your new habit.'

'No, just a slight adjustment to the skirt. Madame Félice promised faithfully before I left her that she would have it delivered to the house the day after tomorrow.'

'That must please you. I know how much you have been longing to ride since our arrival in town.'

'The prospect of doing so has suddenly lost much

of its appeal,' Sophia was not slow to admit, realising that her mother could not have heard the news. 'Clem is leaving us. Which means, of course, that until a replacement can be found I shall be forced to suffer Trapp's presence. And as we both know, Trapp is unfailingly loyal to the head of the family. Everything I say and do will be reported straight back to Papa.'

The Countess could not forbear a smile at the underlying note of pique in her daughter's voice, and turned her head momentarily to stare out of the window.

Like her husband, she too had not been slow to notice that fewer personable gentlemen were paying calls to the house these days, though she could hardly say this had come as any great surprise. She had had a fairly shrewd idea who had been behind those foolish rumours which had circulated on the evening of their very own ball, but which, thankfully, now were dying a natural death. She had noticed, too, during the subsequent days that her daughter's choice of dancing partners had undergone something of a change. There was still a smattering of eligible young men among the favoured few, but these, the Countess strongly suspected, were gentlemen who were not quite ready yet to exchange bachelorhood for wedded bliss.

More amused than annoyed by these rather childish tactics, her ladyship had decided to keep her own counsel, and not take her daughter to task over the mischievous stratagems that she had employed to keep any eligible *parti* at bay, but could not resist saying now, 'But, my dear, I'm certain that you would never do or say anything that might annoy your dear papa,' and then found it was as much as she could do to stop herself laughing outright when Sophia turned to stare resolutely out of the window.

Three days later a message was sent to the stables informing Trapp that Lady Sophia wished her horse to be saddled and brought round from the mews. The head groom received these instructions with mixed feelings: on the one hand he was pleased to learn that Lady Sophia's frisky filly would be receiving some regular exercise at last—she was always far easier to handle when she had been out for an airing; on the other hand, though, he wasn't at all easy in his mind over entrusting the care of the Earl's precious daughter to a virtual stranger. He frowned as he stared at the broad, straight back of his underling, busily engaged in grooming one of his lordship's fine carriage horses, and wondered anew just what to make of Master Benjamin Rudgely.

Trapp himself would have been the first to admit that he could be a hard taskmaster, quick to rebuke, slow to praise. The trouble was, though, he could find no fault with his new subordinate. Master Rudgely had proved to be surprisingly diligent, not once cutting corners in order to get his work over and done with quickly. His handling of horses was a joy to behold, and he tooled the master's town carriage with effortless ease. He had no fault to find with the young man's personal habits either, which had come as something of a relief as they shared the room above the stables, so Trapp could not quite understand why he should continue to have this niggling little doubt in the back of his mind about young Ben.

He scratched his grizzled hair, wondering whether he wasn't just a mite too cynical, just too suspicious of his fellow man. Until his subordinate betrayed the fact that he couldn't be trusted, he ought to be given the benefit of the doubt.

'You can stop what you're doing, lad, and saddle Lady Sophia's filly. The young mistress wishes to ride this morning,' he announced, and didn't notice a pair of blue eyes suddenly flicker with joyful expectation. Which was perhaps just as well, because he would certainly have had second thoughts about allowing the handsome groom to accompany the young mistress out on her ride.

'Now, lad, I want you to listen to what I 'ave to say,' he went on, sitting himself on one of the stools while momentarily pondering over how best to broach the topic of the young mistress's occasionally wayward behaviour. 'I want you to take excellent care of 'er, see. A firm but gentle hand on the reins is what's needed. The master's right fond of 'er, and he wouldn't be best pleased if she came to any harm. So you keep a watchful eye, understand? She can be a mite 'eadstrong on occasions.'

There was a suspicion of a twitch at the corner of

the younger man's mouth. 'I know that, Mr Trapp. I've handled her often enough during the three days I've been here.'

'Eh?' The head groom was startled for a moment, then enlightenment dawned. 'I ain't talking about the filly, you nincompoop!' he snapped testily. 'I knows you can 'andle 'er easy enough. It's Miss Sophia that may cause you problems if she 'appens to be in one of 'er troublesome moods.'

The sight of broad shoulders shaking with suppressed laughter did little for Trapp's peace of mind, and once again doubts assailed him. 'Now, lad, if you feels you ain't up to the job, then I'd rather you say so now, and I'll go with Lady Sophia m'self.'

'Oh, I'm up to it, right enough,' was the prompt response. 'I've had some experience of handling wayward females in my time.'

'Aye, I don't doubt that,' the older man muttered, as a further worrying possibility suddenly occurred to him, and he stared up in troubled silence, scrutinising the undeniably handsome face beneath the beard. 'Just you remember your station, boy, and don't be taking any foolish notions into that head of yours. Miss Sophia's a lady, and you'd best not forget it.'

There was a further moment's silence, then, 'I give you my solemn word that I shall not get ideas above my station, Mr Trapp. I shall treat Lady Sophia just as though she were…my very own sister whenever I accompany her out for a ride.'

'Oh, you will, will you?' The head groom was not

totally reassured and betrayed this fact by a suspicious frown. 'I can't recall your making mention of any sister.'

'Possibly not, but I have one all the same. I've a brother too, as it happens. I was staying with him here in London before I came to you.'

'Strikes me, young Ben, there's a great deal I don't know about you.' Trapp peered owlishly up at him again. 'Why, for instance, did you suddenly take it into your 'ead to leave Jamaica and come back 'ere?'

The answer came promptly enough. 'I'd been out there for five years, and I'd had enough. Homesick, as you might say. Sir Simon Fellows can confirm what I've told you. I can always write to him, and ask him to send a reference to his lordship.'

'Oh, so you can read and write, can you?' Trapp responded, swooping down on this surprising disclosure while at the same time committing the name of Fellows to memory, just in case his lordship should happen to choose at some point in the future to verify Rudgely's bona fides. 'And how came you to be so learned, may I ask?'

The response was not quite so swift in coming this time. 'My—er—old master was keen for me to learn.'

Strangely enough this in no way surprised Trapp, for it had been none other than the Earl who had given of his time when out in India to ensure that Trapp had learned to read and write. Something else, however, did occur to him as peculiar, and he wasn't slow to remark upon it. 'And, I suppose, it were your old master that got you to talk so genteel.'

Once again there was a suspicion of a twitch at the corners of those perfectly sculptured masculine lips. 'I thank you for the compliment, Mr Trapp, but I don't speak that genteel. The old master, though, wouldn't tolerate any cussing when his womenfolk were about, so I suppose I've sort of got out of the habit of using bad words.'

'Well, that ain't no bad thing,' the master of the stables responded fair-mindedly. 'You'll need to mind your tongue when Miss Sophia's about. She's always had the bad habit of remembering words she should never 'ave heard in the first place.' Feeling slightly easier in his mind after the brief talk, Trapp rose to his feet. 'Well, we can't stand about chattering all day. You'd best make haste, lad, and saddle those horses, otherwise the young mistress will be waiting for you.'

The new groom was not slow to obey the brusque command, and had just arrived at the front of the house when the door was thrown wide. A moment later Sophia herself came tripping lightly down the steps, only to stop dead in her tracks, a look of total astonishment on her lovely features.

'Great heavens!' she exclaimed, not attempting to hide her instant recognition. 'So you're my new groom!'

Chapter Four

For the second time in his life Benedict Risely, Seventh Duke of Sharnbrook, experienced that strange bittersweet longing, that intoxicating mixture of tenderness and desire that began somewhere in the region of his loins and spread rapidly through every part of him, sending his pulse rate soaring and his senses reeling. He wanted nothing more than to take her into his arms, and into his bed, to begin to satisfy this earthy powerful craving, and yet all he could do was touch his floppy, misshapen hat in polite acknowledgement, and cup his hands in order to help her into the saddle.

As he mounted the bay, and proceeded to follow at a discreet distance, he began to question, yet again, the wisdom of his actions and wonder what madness had possessed him even to contemplate indulging in such an absurd charade. As a groom his contact with this lovely young creature, who had captured his interest like no other woman had succeeded in doing before, would be frustratingly rare: a mere hour every day if he was lucky. However, given what his brother Nicholas had told him was true, would the Duke of Sharnbrook be better placed to win her regard? At least this way, he decided, he might be granted the opportunity to get to know her a little better without any outside interference or pressures from family and friends; would be given the opportunity to make certain himself whether what he had experienced during those memorable moments in Bond Street, and again now, was something rather more meaningful than mere searing physical attraction that would undoubtedly fade in the passage of time.

He remembered quite clearly that during that tedious sea voyage home he had been granted ample opportunity to think long and hard about the kind of woman he wished to marry. Fortunately the Risely family was a wealthy one, perhaps one of the most affluent in the land. Consequently marriage to an heiress was a consideration which need never weigh with him. His family, of course, would expect him to marry a female of unimpeachable breeding, someone who would know what was expected of her as the Duchess of Sharnbrook, and who would provide him with the sons to carry on the family name.

He, on the other hand, was looking for something rather more than a high-class brood mare in the female he eventually married. He wanted his Duchess to be a helpmate and friend, someone who would share his joys and sorrows, not merely a beautiful adornment to grace the ancestral home. Could Lady Sophia Cleeve turn out to be this perfect companion, this ideal woman whom he had feared he might never be blessed to find?

Glancing over her shoulder, the subject of his thoughts raised one slender hand and beckoned imperiously. 'Come,' she ordered, making the command sound sweetly inviting. 'Come and ride beside me. I wish to speak with you.'

Benedict needed no second prompting, and was beside her in a trice, thinking how magnificent she looked in the severely tailored bottle-green habit, with the cascade of delicate lace adorning her neck, and wondering anew if he were nothing more than a besotted fool to be so enraptured by a lovely face.

'What is your name?'

'Ben, my lady. Benjamin Rudgely,' he answered, repeating the name his resourceful young brother had invented for him.

'And how came you to seek employment with my family, Benjamin Rudgely?' There was a hint of something that sounded suspiciously like disapproval in her pleasant voice. 'Surely Lord Nicholas Risely did not turn you off simply because of that trifling incident in Bond Street the other day?'

Benedict's mind worked rapidly. Evidently she supposed that he had been Nicholas's servant. How his incorrigible young brother would laugh if he ever discovered that!

'Lord Nicholas who?' His feigned bewilderment was worthy of a Drury Lane actor.

'Oh, I see! He just happened along, did he?' Sophia responded, pleased to have this point cleared up. Poor Lord Nicholas had been on the point of plummeting in her estimation. And through no fault of his own either! Her mischievous smile faded as something else rather puzzling occurred to her. 'How came you to hear so quickly that we would be requiring the services of a groom?'

Benedict had decided, when planning this little subterfuge, that the nearer he stuck to the truth when questioned, the easier it would be to maintain his role. It had been a simple matter to persuade his brother's worthy factotum to approach the Earl's groom, and for Figgins to arrange to meet him again at an inn the following evening.

'I happened to be supping a tankard of ale in a tavern not far from here, and overheard a conversation taking place at the next table between your old groom and some other man.' He could sense those green eyes regarding him keenly as he continued to stare straight ahead. 'You see, my lady, I have only recently returned to this country, and have been looking for work, so I felt it couldn't do any harm to take advantage of the situation and ask at your father's stables, just in case the groom did accept the offer made to him.'

She appeared to accept this readily enough, and

after a moment said, 'So, you have been abroad, Ben. What prompted you to return?'

'My old master's death, my lady.' Which was no less than the truth, of course, though he did find it strange referring to his deceased father in that way. He shrugged. 'Besides, I'd been away in Jamaica for five years, and I was keen to see my family again.'

'And does your family reside in London?'

'My brother lives here,' Benedict responded, still determined to stick to the truth as far as possible. He cast a fleeting, sideways glance at his companion, noted the intelligence in striking green eyes, and realised he would be foolish to underestimate her.

He had up until now been very careful to keep his story consistent, but it would not do for him to become over-confident in the role he was playing. Already he had aroused the head groom's suspicions by admitting to the fact that he could read and write, and had foolishly divulged the name of a fellow plantation owner out in Jamaica, but there was little chance of trying to rectify those blunders now. It would not do, however, to drop his guard again, most especially when in this delightful creature's company.

'You must take the opportunity to visit your brother during the time my family remains in London, Ben,' Sophia suggested, after acknowledging the occupants of a passing carriage by raising her crop. 'I shall probably ride most days, weather permitting, but I'm certain you can slip away for an hour or so from time to time to visit members of your family, providing Trapp does not object, of course.'

Again she was betraying that sweet, considerate side to her nature. Benedict stared straight ahead, hiding the glint of admiration in his eyes. He had not forgotten that she had been willing to take her share of the blame after that unforgettable encounter in Bond Street. How many other young females of her class would have concerned themselves unduly over the welfare of a being whom they mistook for a mere servant? Not too many, he felt sure.

'You must not allow our formidable head groom to bully you, Ben,' she continued, an easily discernible hint of devilment in her eyes now. 'He can be a cross-grained old curmudgeon on occasions. The stable-lads back at Jaffrey House are terrified of him.'

'Jaffrey House?' he echoed. 'Is that your country home?'

Sophia nodded. 'The family home in Northamptonshire. My father had it built shortly after his return from India. I and my two younger brothers were born there. It's a lovely place.' Her smile was a trifle wistful. 'It's a great pity that it isn't the Cleeve family's ancestral home, although it is built on land which was once part of the late Earl's estate.'

Memory stirred, and Benedict vaguely recalled his own father mentioning something about the late Earl committing suicide after ruining himself at the gaming tables.

'And who owns the ancestral home now?' he

asked, hoping that for a mere groom he did not seem too inquisitive. Thankfully, she did not appear to think so, although he did note the sudden look of contempt on her face.

'The Marquis of Sywell, a detestable creature of low morals and disgusting habits, whose wanton neglect over the years has resulted in Steepwood Abbey deteriorating into almost a ruin. Papa has offered to buy the place on numerous occasions during the past twenty years, but without success. Fortunately, though, he has managed to regain most of the other properties which once belonged to the Cleeve family, including the town residence.'

They had by this time reached the park. Sophia drew her filly to a halt and gazed about her with scant enthusiasm. It was still more than two weeks before the Season officially began, and yet already the streets and parks were crowded with the rich and famous.

'Look about you, Ben! Isn't it wonderful the way society parades about in its finery for the edification of the populace?' Her sudden shout of laughter was certainly not lacking contempt. 'The Marquis of Sywell is a foul, disgusting member of the human race, but he is in no way unique. Many of those you see here are just as bad. I must remember in future to ride earlier in the day when the air is less contaminated.'

So Nicholas had not been exaggerating, after all, Benedict mused, as he proceeded to follow again at a discreet distance. Lady Sophia Cleeve truly harboured a deal of contempt for her own class. His task, it seemed, was going to prove to be far more formidable than he had at first supposed!

That evening the Earl, still determined to attend the occasional party, escorted his wife and daughter to the ball being held by the Marquis and Marchioness of Strattan. If the formidable matron harboured any ill-will at being passed over by a certain famous *modiste* a few days before, she certainly betrayed no sign of it as she graciously welcomed the young lady who had received preferential treatment, a circumstance which the Countess herself was not slow to remark upon once her husband had drifted away into the room set out for cards.

'But isn't it considered vulgar for women of our class to give vent to their feelings in public, Mama? I know some do, while others...' Sophia's eyes drifted towards a young woman whose husband had been quite openly indulging in an amorous affair with a notorious Cyprian since his arrival in town '...manage to hide their emotions quite remarkably well.'

Her ladyship followed the direction of her daughter's gaze. She too had heard rumours of Lord Rochford's torrid affair, and felt a great deal of sympathy for his pretty young wife, whose behaviour in public was faultless. 'Not all marriages turn out so badly, Sophia.'

'No, Mama. I know they do not. But I suspect a great many ladies here tonight have at some time or other been forced to suffer in silence over their husbands' peccadilloes. I rather fear that, my nature being what it is, I should not be so tolerant.'

The Countess thought it wisest to change the subject and, catching sight of her friend and neighbour, Lady Elizabeth Perceval, sitting with her daughter, guided Sophia towards them.

'I'm so pleased you accepted this invitation tonight,' Robina said, when her mother's attention was being held by the Countess. 'It seems ages since I last saw you. What have you been doing with yourself?'

'Oh, nothing particularly exciting,' Sophia responded, sublimely ignoring the fact that she had not spent a single evening at home since the night of her own ball.

'I do not believe that for a moment,' Robina countered, suddenly feeling much more relaxed, just as she always did whenever Sophia was about. 'Everywhere Mama and I go we hear your name mentioned. Why, only the other day we heard some silly rumour about you wishing to marry one of your papa's footmen.'

Robina's amusement faded the instant she detected a certain glint in a pair of green eyes, a look she had seen too many times in the past not to know precisely what it signified. 'Oh, Sophia! Surely you didn't start that silly rumour about yourself as well? Your father will be furious if he ever finds out.'

'Yes, I expect he probably would be,' Sophia agreed. There could be no denying that the Earl had always been very indulgent where she was concerned, far more so than with any one of her brothers, and yet she knew that even with her his patience was not limitless.

'Unfortunately, Robina, unlike you, I do not always behave as I ought. I'm very well aware that back home in the Abbey villages it is a commonly held belief that I've been thoroughly spoilt and indulged. Which is no less than the truth, of course,' she agreed, with the honesty that was so much a part of her charm. 'I hate being thwarted. It's a failing, I know, and one I really must try to overcome. My only excuse is that I didn't precisely say that I intended marrying a footman, merely that in general I prefer the company of servants to that of more privileged members of society.'

She paused for a moment while she considered the painted figures on her fan. 'Which, strangely enough, has turned out to be true. I went riding this afternoon in the company of my groom, and can honestly say that I felt perfectly contented for the first time since arriving in town.'

Robina didn't find this in the least surprising. 'Oh, well,' she shrugged. 'That's only to be expected. I know you look upon Clem as more of a friend than a servant.'

'It wasn't Clem who accompanied me,' Sophia informed her, staring sightlessly across the ballroom, her mind's eye conjuring up a clear image of a tall and powerfully built man, with his long mane of thick golden-brown hair and penetrating blue eyes. 'Clem, sadly, has left us to take charge of the stables at an estate somewhere in the south of England, I believe.'

Robina was shocked to learn this and hardly knew what to say. The inhabitants of the four Abbey villages had grown accustomed over the years to seeing the Earl of Yardley's daughter riding over the Northamptonshire countryside in the company of her trusty groom. For years Clem had been Sophia's loyal companion. It would seem most strange no longer seeing them riding about together.

'I know you must have been terribly upset at losing him,' she said at length, genuine sympathy edging her voice.

'Very,' Sophia agreed, smiling wryly. 'Spoilt I may be, Robin, but not so selfish as to try to prevent someone I like from bettering himself. It will be some years yet before our head groom is ready to retire, and Clem is more than capable of running a stable. I must confess, though, I was very favourably impressed with Clem's replacement,' she went on to divulge, after her attention had just for one moment been captured by two gentlemen sitting together on the opposite side of the room. She shook her head. 'It was so strange. At the time I wasn't aware of it, but when I arrived back at the house, and thought about the conversation we'd had during our ride, I realised that it hadn't seemed as if I'd been conversing with a servant at all.'

Again Robina wasn't unduly surprised. 'You always did chatter away quite happily to Clem,' she reminded her.

'Very true. Somehow, though, this seemed different. I found myself agreeing with almost everything he said, especially remarks he made about our own class.' She laughed at the absurdity of being instructed by a groom on the correct way to behave. 'Silly, really. Perhaps it was just that I felt totally relaxed in his company.'

Robina did not think it at all silly. 'I know what you mean. There are those, even servants, with whom you instantly experience a rapport.' She gave vent to a heartfelt sigh. 'I know Mama and Papa wish me to make a good match. Oh, but I would much rather marry someone with whom I felt comfortable, who didn't expect me to behave correctly all the time, and would accept me as I am!'

Sophia's gaze automatically strayed towards the lady sitting on her friend's right. She didn't doubt for a moment that Robina's upbringing at the vicarage in Abbot Quincey had been happy for the most part. It could not, however, have been easy living up to Lady Elizabeth Perceval's exacting standards of behaviour.

Lady Elizabeth was well respected in all four of the Abbey villages. She had proved the perfect companion and helpmate to Abbot Quincey's hard-working and kindly vicar. Her own efforts on behalf of the poor and needy were as tireless as her husband's, and she had never been too proud to enter the humblest of abodes in order to offer some comfort to the sick and dying. Yet there remained an imperious air about her that never failed to remind one and all of her noble birth and that they were in the presence of the daughter of a duke.

Sophia could only assume that Lady Elizabeth's upbringing had been a strict one, for the vicar's wife had certainly instilled rigid standards of behaviour in her daughters, most especially in Robina, who, being the eldest, had been expected to set an example to her three younger sisters. No easy task to be forced to conform to such high ideals, Sophia mused, her gaze once more travelling about the large and now well-filled ballroom, and she could not help wondering just how much of her sweet-natured friend's character had been suppressed over the years, and what surprising traits might surface if ever dear Robina was removed for any length of time from her strict mama's sphere.

'Tell me, Robin, do you happen to know who that dark-haired gentleman is sitting across the room with Lord Byron? I do not believe I've ever seen him before.'

Robina, having a remarkable memory for names and faces, was able to enlighten her at once. 'Sir Lucius Crawley. He has only recently arrived in town. Although,' she added in an undertone, 'I think there must be something quite unsavoury about him, for Mama said, after I had stood up with him just once at a party the other night, that on no account was I to do so again.'

'How very interesting!' The telltale glint which

preceded some outrageous utterance or action on Sophia's part appeared in her eyes. 'I expect he's a rake.'

Robina's spontaneous chortle earned her a look of mild reproof from her punctilious mama, but help was at hand in the form of her equally meticulous cousin, Hugo Perceval, who came across to request her as his partner in the next set of country dances.

As she followed their progress on to the floor, Sophia noticed the strikingly attractive Sir Lucius Crawley rise to his feet and begin to saunter across the room in her direction. If his intention had been to claim her for his partner he was destined to be disappointed, for Lord Nicholas Risely, appearing from nowhere, was suddenly standing before her, politely requesting that she partner him in the next dance.

As the young lord continued to rein supreme amongst that group of 'safe' admirers, Sophia did not hesitate. She always found him amusing, his witty remarks coming as a welcome relief after the studied politeness she was usually forced to endure from most other gentlemen. He was a fount of wisdom too, always able to regale her with the latest *on-dits*, and what he did not know about the famous and infamous who moved in the highest circles really wasn't worth knowing. Consequently she did not hesitate to tax him about the strikingly handsome man who had succeeded in capturing her interest.

'Has Crawley arrived in town?' Betraying faint surprise, Nicholas glanced about him and quickly caught sight of the Baronet, whose reputation was, to say the least, slightly unsavoury. 'Ah, yes! So he has. Doesn't usually arrive before the beginning of the Season. Can only assume that he must be contemplating matrimony again.'

'Again?' Sophia echoed, intrigued.

Nicholas was longing to discover how his brother went on, for he had not seen or heard from Benedict since he had adopted the guise of a groom. Realising, however, that a sudden change in the topic of conversation would appear most odd, and not quite knowing how to broach the subject of stable-hands anyway, he thought it wisest to satisfy the roguish Lady Sophia's curiosity with regard to Sir Lucius.

'Yes, he married some "golden dolly" a few years ago in order to save the ancestral home. Mortgaged up to the hilt, so I was led to believe. Still,' he shrugged, 'not surprising he got himself in high water. A bit of a loose screw is Sir Lucius, m'dear. Not a man to deprive himself of his pleasures, as you might say.'

Sophia had discovered over the years that one learned a great deal more if one refrained from prying too hard. She had also discovered that gentlemen were far less inhibited in their choice of language if not continually asked what they meant. So, committing Lord Nicholas's more colourful vocabulary to memory, she merely said, 'And I presume his first wife died.'

'Giving birth to a stillborn child within a year of

their marriage, if my memory serves me correctly. Lucky escape, if you ask me,' he remarked, with a tactless disregard for the poor young woman's tragic demise. 'Common knowledge that he only married her for the money. Made that plain enough by resorting to his old ways within weeks of the marriage taking place.'

Disappointed, but not unduly surprised, Sophia's interest swiftly began to wane. If what Lord Nicholas had told her was true, then it appeared that Sir Lucius, a profligate with no thought for anyone but himself, epitomised what she most despised in her class.

Ordinarily she wouldn't have given the Baronet another thought, but as the last strains of music died away, and the couples began to leave the floor, she discovered Sir Lucius, evidently not a man to be thwarted in his objectives a second time, standing before her. Lord Nicholas had little choice but to make the introductions before he moved away, leaving Sophia to stare up into a pair of striking blue eyes, deeply set in a thin, but not unattractive, masculine countenance.

She could not help comparing the faintly mocking eyes that stared unblinkingly down at her with another pair of the same striking hue which had regarded her keenly from time to time earlier that day. She recalled quite clearly that there had been a directness in Ben Rudgely's gaze, but at least his blue orbs had left her fully clad, whereas now she felt as if she had just been divested of her chemise, and her charms were being ruthlessly scrutinised for any slight flaw.

She smiled to herself as, after a brief exchange of pleasantries, they took up their positions in the set. Undoubtedly a great many women would be attracted by Sir Lucius's darkly brooding good looks and provocative gaze, but Sophia could detect a distinct lack of warmth in the smiling, thin-lipped mouth, and a hint of something faintly sinister in his whole demeanour which made her very certain that any woman would be a fool to place her well-being into the hands of this man.

In this, at least, she and her father were in perfect accord. Although he had visited the capital rarely during the past few years, the Earl had kept abreast of society's comings and goings, and had learned something of Sir Lucius's tainted reputation. Consequently he was not best pleased, after paying his brief visit to the card-room, to discover his beloved daughter in the disreputable Baronet's company.

Quickly locating the whereabouts of his wife, he did not hesitate to draw her a little to one side and give voice to his displeasure by demanding to know what she was about in allowing their daughter to stand up with a man of Sir Lucius Crawley's stamp.

'My dear, I was hardly in a position to do much about it,' she responded in her calm way, while suspecting that he had been keeping a watchful eye on proceedings from the first. 'He approached Sophia before she had left the floor with Lord Nicholas Risely.'

Momentarily diverted, he said, 'Risely?' He had thought that there had been something vaguely familiar in the tall, blond-haired young man who had danced with Sophia first. 'What, one of old Sharnbrook's brood, is he?'

'Yes, the younger son. Sophia is quite fond of him.'

'Is she indeed?' Hope stirred, but was quickly dashed by his Countess's assurance that friendship was all that Sophia felt for the late duke's younger son.

'He's an endearing young scamp. I'm very fond of him myself,' she went on to confess, 'but he wouldn't suit Sophia at all. He's far too young. So I would be most obliged if you did not try to promote a union between them.'

'I wouldn't dream of interfering, my love,' he assured her, but she was not wholly convinced, and betrayed the fact by raising a decidedly sceptical brow.

'Then why, pray, did you suddenly take it into your head to accompany us this evening, if it was not to keep an eye on our daughter? If you consider me an inadequate chaperon, Thomas, then I would suggest that you employ a suitable duenna,' she suggested bluntly, but without rancour. None the less his lordship took note of the mild reproof.

'Now, now, dear,' he said soothingly. 'You know full well that there is no one I would trust more with the care of our daughter than you. It's just…it's just…'

'It's just that you are concerned for our only daughter's well-being,' she finished for him, smiling in spite of the fact that she considered he worried unnecessarily. 'I love Sophia no less than you do, Thomas, but unlike you I have far more faith in our daughter's judgement. Sooner or later I believe that she will meet a gentleman whom she would be happy to marry, and, moreover, a gentleman whom we shall find perfectly acceptable. But until such time, if you take my advice, you will let well alone, and permit our far from obtuse daughter to enjoy her first Season.'

Chapter Five

Resolved to take her exercise long before the park became congested with fops and dandies, and sporting-mad gentlemen bent on displaying their skills on horseback or in their racing carriages, Sophia rose early the following morning and was pleased to discover, as her maid threw back the drapes, that the day looked set to remain fair.

She was convinced that the mounting excitement bubbling up inside, as she broke her fast and then hurriedly scrambled into her habit, stemmed purely and simply from the pleasure she would attain from having the park virtually to herself. So she was at a loss to understand why her spirits should suddenly plummet when, a short while later, her new groom's only response to her bright smile and cheerful good morning was the merest nod of his head.

Being singularly lacking in conceit, Sophia would never have supposed for a moment that the mere sight of her could reduce a self-possessed gentleman into little more than a languishing dolt who seemed to spend half his time these days staring into space, longing for that moment when he could call her his own, and his nights dreaming that she was lying in his arms, a willing recipient of his lovemaking, only to wake and find himself frustratingly alone.

She would never have supposed, either, that the man bending before her, hands cupped in readiness to toss her into the saddle, was doing his utmost to keep an iron control over his emotions and frustrations. She only knew that she was feeling unaccountably hurt by her new groom's seeming indifference to her presence, and stared down at the bent head, wondering how her perfect companion of yesterday could turn overnight into some surly dullard who could not bring himself even to pass the time of day.

After a few moments, when she made not the least attempt to place her slender foot in his hands, Ben raised his head, a question in his eyes. 'Have you changed your mind, my lady? Do you not wish to go riding this morning?'

'Now, is that not strange!' she remarked, with more than just a hint of sarcasm coating her every word. 'I was about to ask you the same question.'

He straightened to tower above her, his expression guarded. 'I do not perfectly understand you, m'lady.'

'No?' Sophia wasn't at all convinced that this was true, for the intelligence she could easily perceive in those striking blue eyes told a different story.

Imps of mischief began to dance in her own. 'Then

let me make myself perfectly clear. I believe I'm generally held to be a most unexacting mistress, but even I'm not above dealing a sound box round the ear to any servant who shows reluctance in carrying out the few services I might demand of him.'

It was at this precise moment that the filly chose to demonstrate her impatience to be off. Ben's muttered, 'Unruly little baggage!' had her calmed in a trice, but Sophia wasn't at all certain that the mild admonition had been directed at her horse. She decided to give him the benefit of the doubt over this, but wasn't feeling generous enough to permit his subdued state to pass without explanation and demanded, as they rode out of the square, why he appeared to be out of sorts that morning.

'And please do not insult my intelligence by telling me that there's nothing wrong,' she went on. 'You've a face like a wet Friday.'

Benedict could not prevent a smile. His little darling evidently was not one to mince words. But how on earth could he tell her that she was the cause of all his present troubles, and that he was simply a frustrated man?

'If I appear a little—er—diffident, my lady, then you must forgive me and put it down to inexperience, and my desire not to be found wanting. I have not always been a groom, you see,' he admitted, consoling himself with the knowledge that at least this much was true.

'What kind of work were you engaged in before?'

she asked and, prepared, he was ready with the answer.

'I have performed many duties in my time, my
lady. I was born in the country, and am quite accustomed to working with various animals, not just
horses.'

'A farm boy, eh?'

'Er—no, not quite, my lady. I was born on a large
estate in Hampshire, and worked from time to time
on the home farm when I was much younger.'

How very interesting! Sophia mused, eyes narrow-
ing as she studied the handsome profile, with its high,
intelligent forehead, the faintly aquiline nose and the
strong line of the square jaw. He might dress and
vaguely sound like a yokel, but he was certainly no
country bumpkin. Rustics didn't use words like 'accustomed' and 'diffident'. There was far more to
Master Benjamin Rudgely than met the eye!

'So, what prompted you to go to the West Indies,
Ben?' Her voice was light, pleasantly conversational,
yet Benedict could easily detect the note of keen interest barely concealed. Her curiosity, quite understandably, was well and truly roused, and he had
every intention of satisfying her inquisitiveness with
the truth as far as he dared.

'My old master ordered me to go, my lady. I cannot
in truth say that I wished to leave England,' he divulged, recalling his resentment quite clearly, 'but I
have to own that my time in Jamaica taught me a lot.'

Although continuing to stare straight ahead,

Benedict was well aware that he was being regarded rather closely. He waited for the next searching question, and was faintly surprised when she merely remarked that he must have observed many changes since his return.

'Some here in the capital, certainly. Many new buildings have been erected since I was last here. And, of course, you have the new gas lighting in this part of the city.' He swiftly glimpsed a less impressive sight. 'Some things, however, have not improved in the least.'

Sophia followed the direction of his gaze in time to see a beadle chasing two poverty-stricken children round a corner into a side street. There were poor everywhere, but one tended to notice them particularly here in London, where the gap between the classes seemed even more marked. The authorities did their best to keep the streets in this part of the city free from beggars, but they were fighting a losing battle; there were just too many of them.

'London's shame,' she murmured, experiencing a surge of sympathy.

'Mankind's shame,' he corrected. 'And mankind has a great deal of which it need be ashamed.'

They had by this time reached the entrance to the park, and Benedict changed the subject by remarking how pleasant it was to have the place almost to themselves. His delightful companion wholeheartedly agreed, and he could easily detect the wistful note in her voice, and knew precisely what was passing through that delightfully wilful little head of hers.

'How unfortunate that it isn't permitted to enjoy a good gallop in the park!' He slanted a mocking glance as she turned startled eyes in his direction. 'Oh, yes, my lady. Lowly groom I may be, but even I know that ladies are permitted to ride only at a sedate trot while in the capital.'

'A timely reminder!' she exclaimed, gurgling with laughter. 'How very glad I am that I have you to instruct me in how to go on.' Those imps of mischief, always lurking beneath the surface, added a distinct sparkle to her eyes. 'You missed your vocation in life, Benjamin Rudgely. You ought to have been a duenna.'

He almost choked. How dared she suggest that he ally himself to that species which he had found an utter bane in his younger days! Her gurgle of laughter at his affronted expression quickly faded, and he turned his head in the direction of her suddenly perturbed gaze.

In the years he had spent abroad many of society's lesser personages had faded from his memory, but Benedict had little difficulty in recognising the lone figure approaching on a showy chestnut gelding.

He would have been the first to admit that he had never been, and possibly never would be, a paragon of all the virtues. He'd certainly been no angel in his younger days. Long sessions of drinking and gambling had not been, he was ashamed to say, rare occurrences. Nor had it been unusual to see him about the town with a ravishing beauty on his arm. His liaisons, if not precisely discreetly conducted, had without exception been with women of his own class or with those who knew the rules. He had never tampered with innocence, nor had any one of the ladies with whom he had enjoyed more intimate relations suffered as a consequence of her association with him. Which was a great deal more than could be said for several young women whose names had been linked with that of Sir Lucius Crawley.

One particularly unsavoury tale involving the Baronet instantly sprang into Benedict's mind. The young lady involved in the affair had come from a good family, and rumour had had it at the time that she was destined to come into a considerable sum of money upon her marriage. Soon after her arrival in town the poor girl had fallen under the destructive spell of Sir Lucius and had agreed to an elopement. Fortunately the young woman had not been without male protectors. Her uncle, in hot pursuit, had managed to overtake the runaways some twenty miles north of London and, certain that Sir Lucius had been nothing more than a fortune-hunter, had not hesitated to inform the Baronet that his niece would not inherit a penny unless she married with her family's consent. This, of course, had changed everything. Sir Lucius had returned to town, and the poor broken-hearted young woman had cast herself from an upper-storey window at her uncle's home a few days later and had died instantly.

Unfortunately that poor deluded girl was by no means the only fair damsel to suffer as a consequence of trusting the self-seeking Baronet. So it came as something of a relief to Benedict, as he fell back a few paces to allow Sir Lucius to manoeuvre his mount alongside Sophia's filly, to discover that his darling girl did not appear in the least susceptible to Sir Lucius's darkly brooding good looks, though she managed to greet him cordially enough by remarking that she was rather surprised to see him out and about at this time of day.

'Truth to tell, my lady, I do not make a habit of rising at this ungodly hour when residing in town,' he admitted, his dark gaze devouring her every curve, and making Sophia thankful that she was wearing extra layers of clothing that morning. 'But I was fortunate enough to overhear you mention to that pretty little friend of yours that you intended riding early this morning, and could not let such a golden opportunity of furthering our acquaintance slip through my fingers.'

So he was not above doing a spot of eavesdropping when it suited his purposes. And what was his intention? Sophia couldn't help wondering. Seduction? No, she doubted that very much. A womaniser he undoubtedly was, but he would not risk being ostracised by society by foolishly attempting to ruin the daughter of an earl.

She regarded him in silence for a moment, her gaze far less flattering than his own. Perhaps Lord Nicholas had been correct in his assumption, and Sir Lucius was once again contemplating matrimony. Perhaps he was even considering her as a possible candidate for the future Lady Crawley. If so, she would swiftly disabuse him. Not for the world would she ally herself to a person who would, she didn't doubt, in the years to come turn out to be a mirror image of that debauched roué the Marquis of Sywell!

'You flatter me, sir, but you should have saved yourself the trouble. I'm certain that our paths will cross from time to time during the forthcoming weeks.'

This was not precisely the reaction to which he had grown accustomed over the years when paying a certain lady particular attention, but Sir Lucius was not deterred. Experience told him that Lady Sophia, for all her self-possessed air, was a complete innocent when it came to the gentle art of dalliance. Added to which, he had always found the chase far more exciting than the inevitable surrender, and knew that he would attain the utmost pleasure in taming this spirited little minx and bending her to his will.

'And I would consider it a great favour,' Sophia continued, disliking the way he continued to regard her, like some ravenous dog drooling over a bone, 'if you did not make it generally known that I prefer to take my exercise at this time of day, sir. My morning rides are sacrosanct periods when I can enjoy a little solitude.'

A deep masculine rumble, only partially suppressed, reached her ears, and it took every ounce of self-control Sophia possessed not to laugh outright herself when Sir Lucius swung round in the saddle to cast her highly amused groom a darkling look. She knew she ought to take Ben roundly to task for riding so close and shamelessly listening to every word of the conversation, but she had no intention of doing so, now or later, for she sensed that as long as Benjamin Rudgely was at hand she need never fear a man of Sir Lucius Crawley's stamp.

'I sincerely trust that you do not consider my presence this morning an intrusion, my lady,' the Baronet said smoothly, though he couldn't quite disguise his lingering annoyance at the insulting servant's behaviour. 'You were certainly not averse to my company last night, as I recall.'

Sophia silently cursed herself for every kind of fool for paying Sir Lucius particular attention at the Strattans' ball. She had known that it would be a mistake to dance with him a second time, and yet she had foolishly done so, simply because earlier in the evening she had glimpsed an expression on her father's face that informed her clearly enough that he did not approve.

Although her experience of men most certainly was not vast, some inner feminine wisdom warned her that Sir Lucius could be a dangerous man if crossed, and one, moreover, who would not take kindly to being made to look a fool. So it would be far better, surely, she decided quickly, to make her feelings clear now, rather than allow further misunderstandings to occur in the future. Yet, for some obscure reason, and for the life of her she couldn't understand why, she just didn't want Ben to know how very foolish she had been to offer a man of Sir Lucius's reputation encouragement, minimal though it had been.

They had by this time reached a very secluded area of the park. 'Shall we stroll for a while?' she suggested, drawing rein by a clump of trees, and slipping lightly to the ground before either Ben or Sir Lucius could assist her.

She did not notice the disapproving look that flickered in a pair of alert blue eyes as she wandered beneath the canopy of branches, but Sir Lucius most certainly did, and it gave him a deal of satisfaction to order the groom to remain with the horses.

Coming to a halt by a sturdy elm, Sophia waited for Sir Lucius to join her. 'I believe I owe you an apology, sir,' she announced, coming straight to the point and sounding far more composed than she was in fact feeling. She had not meant to walk quite so far, and Ben seemed a disturbingly long way away.

'Apologise, my dear?' Sir Lucius, his eyes glinting with satisfaction, and with something far more disturbing that Sophia didn't choose to define, took a step closer. 'Apologise for what, pray? You have done me no disservice,' he purred silkily. 'Quite the contrary, I assure you.'

Sophia instinctively took a step away, only to find her back pressed against the trunk of the elm. What had seemed quite a simple task a few minutes ago had assumed alarming proportions. Sir Lucius was no easily managed callow youth whose desires could be suppressed by a few well-chosen words. He was a master at the art of dalliance; undoubtedly a man whose success with women over the years prompted him to pursue a particular quarry remorselessly if given sufficient reason to suppose that his attentions would not in the end be wholly unwelcome. And hadn't she foolishly offered him sufficient encouragement already by leading him to this secluded spot?

He confirmed her worst fears by moving a step nearer and placing one shapely hand on the trunk by her head. Faint-hearted she had never been, not even as a child, and it would have afforded her the utmost satisfaction to administer a resounding box round the ears when he lowered his eyes and unashamedly contemplated the bodice of her habit. She didn't suppose for a moment that an assurance from her that she was completely indifferent to him would be believed, and she began to wonder just how she could manage to extricate herself from this embarrassing predicament when she clearly detected the sound of a twig snapping nearby.

Sir Lucius heard it too, and swung round sharply. Unlike Sophia, it was not profound relief that he was experiencing at discovering the groom standing a matter of three feet away, as he betrayed clearly enough by his rasping demand to know what he thought he was doing. 'I believe I told you to remain with the horses,' he growled between clenched teeth.

'You did,' Benedict confirmed smoothly and, as far as Sophia could detect, completely unperturbed by the Baronet's display of hostility. If he betrayed anything at all, it was a trace of exasperation when he glanced briefly in her direction. 'But might I remind you that I'm not your lackey and, therefore, am not prepared to take orders from you.'

Then everything happened so quickly that Sophia could only utter a startled gasp in dismay. Sir Lucius, cursing under his breath, raised his crop, but Ben easily warded off the blow aimed at his shoulder, and a second later delivered a powerful hit to the jaw which had the Baronet sprawling on the ground.

'What the devil's going on here?' an authoritative and very familiar voice demanded to know, and Sophia, utterly stunned by what had taken place, was unable to believe the evidence of her own eyes as she saw her elder brother stalking purposefully towards them.

If she had possessed the power to make herself invisible she most certainly would have made good use of it. She didn't suppose for a moment that Marcus honestly required an explanation, and as her tongue seemed to have decided to attach itself to the roof of her mouth, she found herself completely unequal to the task of offering any.

She watched as her brother's astute gaze went from Ben, who looked ready, and more than willing, to repeat his actions of a few moments before, to Sir Lucius who, still appearing slightly dazed, was making an attempt to rise.

'Allow me to assist you, Crawley,' he said, only to have his helping hand thrust irritably aside.

'You'll permit me to inform you, Angmering,' Sir Lucius remarked, when he was at last on his feet again, and doing his best to repair his slightly dishevelled appearance by brushing the leaves from his jacket, 'that your father's choice of servants leaves much to be desired.'

'So it would seem,' Marcus responded, glancing once again in the groom's direction. 'None the less, you'll allow me to point out, Crawley, that we are not in the habit of whipping our people. From what I observed, this man reacted in self-defence. So might I suggest that we forget the whole unfortunate incident and go our separate ways before we attract the attention of the vulgarly curious.'

Sophia realised by Sir Lucius's suddenly alert expression as he gazed about him that her shrewd brother had said precisely the right thing. The Baronet's temper might be hasty, he might even enjoy the notoriety his amorous exploits had brought him over the years, but she doubted very much that he would risk being ostracised by the Ton by making a vulgar spectacle of himself in a public place. There had been no one in sight a few minutes before. This, however, was no longer the case, for a small cluster of riders was now heading down the path in their direction.

'You are quite right, of course, Angmering.' Swooping to retrieve his hat, which still lay among the leaves, Crawley cast an unmistakably vindictive glance in the groom's direction. 'I just hope my memory proves as amenable as yours,' and with that, and the briefest of nods, he was gone.

'Now perhaps you'll be good enough to inform me what the deuce that was all about!' Marcus demanded, easily detecting his sister's faint sigh of relief.

Ten years her senior he may have been, but Sophia had never been in awe of her frequently abrupt elder brother. Flashing him a look from beneath her lashes, which informed him clearly enough that she was beginning to regain her equilibrium and was not best pleased with his cavalier attitude, she turned to Ben, who continued to appear quite remarkably unconcerned in the circumstances. 'You return to Berkeley Square now. My brother, I'm sure, will see me safely home. And, Ben,' she added softly, when he turned to go. 'Thank you.'

'Who the deuce is that fellow, Sophie?' Marcus was not slow to enquire once Ben was safely out of earshot. 'Strangely enough he reminds me of someone, but for the life of me I cannot think who it can be.' He shook his head as though dismissing it from his mind. 'And why wasn't Clem with you?'

'Clem has left us to work for someone else. My new groom's name is Benjamin Rudgely.'

'Is it by gad!' The name meant absolutely nothing to Marcus. 'Well, Benjamin Rudgely will not be your groom for very much longer if he continues to conduct himself in such a fashion,' he warned. 'A menial cannot go round flooring his betters and expect to retain his position.'

Sophia couldn't understand why, but she took great exception to having her new groom labelled a menial and was not slow to voice her displeasure. 'Furthermore, Marcus, I shall not hear of Ben being dismissed because of this morning's unfortunate occurrence. You saw yourself what happened.'

'I saw, right enough,' he confirmed, as they returned to the horses, 'but I cannot understand for the life of me why it should have occurred.'

'It happened because I was foolish enough to pay Crawley attention last night. I certainly didn't invite him to come riding with me this morning,' she hurriedly assured him, accepting his help to get into the saddle, and easily detecting the reproachful glint in his dark eyes as he mounted his own fine bay, 'but evidently he must have supposed that his presence would not be unwelcome. I was trying to think of some delicate way of informing him that rakes were not to my taste when Ben suddenly appeared.'

She decided to be fair and give Sir Lucius the benefit of the doubt. 'I don't suppose for a moment that Crawley would contemplate a seduction scene here in the park, but I cannot deny that I was very glad that Ben was with me. And now, Marcus, all I wish to do is forget the whole unfortunate episode.'

He looked as if he was about to say something in response, but then, evidently, thought better of it, and they rode towards the park gates in silence, until Sophia asked him when he had arrived in town.

'Late yesterday evening. I'm staying with my friend Lawrence Petersham. We'll be here for a few days, and then we're travelling to his country home in Hampshire to do a spot of shooting and fishing.'

Disappointed, but not unduly surprised, Sophia cast her brother a thoughtful glance. Marcus never attempted to make use of the town house in Berkeley Square when the Earl was in residence, preferring instead to put up at a hotel or stay with friends. During the past few years his visits to Jaffrey House had been less frequent too, and she could not help feeling that as long as he continued to avoid their father's company whenever possible, any resentment he might continue to harbour with regard to the ill-treatment he considered his mother had received at the Earl's hands would continue to fester deep inside.

As the Earl had always flatly refused to discuss anything about his first marriage, and the Countess, loyal to the last, had not betrayed his trust by divulging any of the details, Sophia had never been in possession of all the facts and she doubted very much that Marcus had either.

Childhood memories began to filter through her mind, and she recalled vividly that lovely summer day, almost eleven years ago, when she had peered out of one of the upper-floor windows at Jaffrey House and had spotted her brother heading across the park in the direction of Steepwood Abbey. The grounds especially had always held a certain fascination for him, and he had frequently gone there to be private with his thoughts.

Sophia herself had never been similarly drawn to either the Abbey or its grounds, not even as a child. Many eerie stories about the place had been passed down through the centuries. In more recent years the Marquis of Sywell's debauched activities had been sufficient to dissuade most young females from venturing there alone, and Sophia, not always the most obedient of children, had for once adhered to her parents' strict command and had never once attempted to venture into the Abbey grounds on her own. Having her elder brother's protection, however, had made a visit perfectly in order, and she had not hesitated on that long-ago summer's day in escaping from her governess in order to follow him.

Marcus, having been something of a taciturn youth, had not been best pleased to discover his young sister racing across the park in his direction. When she had finally reached his side, he had made his feelings brutally clear by ordering her to return home in no uncertain terms and, her nature being what it was, she had flatly refused. A heated argument had ensued, which had culminated in Marcus saying some rather unkind things about their father, and she retaliating by flying at him, small fists making contact with any part of his anatomy she could reach, while screaming insults about his mother. Marcus had swiftly captured her flailing arms, and when eventually she had grown calmer they had made a pact: never again would he say unkind things about their father and in return Sophia had promised never to pass a derogatory remark about his mother.

During the ensuing years they had both kept to the bargain. Sophia had no intention of breaking her promise now by informing him that she considered his continued avoidance of their father's company very foolish, and merely voiced the hope that she would be seeing something of him during his short sojourn in town.

'I should imagine that highly likely,' he announced, and then promptly lessened her delight by adding, 'It's quite obvious that you need someone to keep an eye on you, my girl.'

Sophia could feel her occasionally ungovernable temper begin to stir. She was still feeling very guilty, but steadfastly refused to be held entirely responsible for what had occurred. 'I shall take leave to inform you, Marcus, that I neither desire nor require your services as a chaperon,' she hissed, putting him in mind of a pettish kitten. 'I should go on a great deal better if the male members of my family ceased to meddle in my affairs.'

'Ha!' Marcus barked, not slow to understand. 'So Father's been laying down the law, has he? High time too!'

'I might have expected some such tactless response from you!' she retorted, thoroughly nettled now. 'I only hope that when you finally decide that it's time for you to settle down and marry he'll lay down the law in your choice of partner too!'

'So, that's the way of it, is it?' Wicked though his smile undoubtedly was, it did contain a trace of sympathy. 'Come on, Sophie, be fair,' he urged gently. 'I would be the first to admit that I haven't always agreed with everything he's ever done or said, but I'm sure Father has only your best interests at heart. The last thing he would want is for you to fall prey to some fortune-hunter.'

'I'm not a complete widgeon, Marcus. I do realise that. What you and Papa fail to realise, however, is that I'm no longer a child, and am quite capable of making the reasoned choice when it comes to selecting a husband.'

He seemed decidedly unconvinced, as his next words proved. 'You may consider yourself up to snuff, my girl, but I'm afraid your behaviour this morning rather refutes that. No female in her right mind would ever offer a man of Crawley's stamp a h'a'porth of encouragement.'

They had by this time reached Berkeley Square,

and Sophia, not waiting for assistance, slipped down from the saddle. The fact that there was more than an element of truth in what he had just said only succeeded in annoying her further, and she could not resist wiping away his smugly satisfied smile by announcing, 'You may be certain of one thing, Marcus, a green girl I still might be on occasions, but not so foolish as ever to become tied for life to an overbearing, arrogant bore such as you!'

Half amused, half annoyed by what he considered a totally inaccurate assessment of his character, Marcus walked the horses round to the mews. His little sister, it seemed, had not yet learned to curb that temper of hers, nor had she completely abandoned her wilful ways.

'What she needs, of course, is a firm hand. I sincerely hope her future husband will be a man who won't be afraid to school her when necessary,' he muttered, with a certain grim satisfaction, only half aware that he had spoken his thoughts aloud.

'The right sort of man could handle her easily enough, sir,' an amused voice remarked.

'You may be right, but I for one will pity the poor devil, whoever he may be,' Marcus responded, automatically handing over the reins to the new groom. 'She can be an unruly little madam when the mood takes her.'

'Can't say I'm surprised. It's quite obvious she was spoilt as a child. The Earl's fault, I suspect.'

'There you have the right of it! If he had been

firmer in his dealings with Sophie years ago, she wouldn't have turned out to be such a—' Marcus caught himself up abruptly, suddenly realising to whom he was speaking, and cast Ben a frowning glance. 'I'd advise you to keep your opinions to yourself, my man!' he snapped, but was unable to prevent a smile as he stalked into the house. Impertinent the groom might be, but he was certainly no fool and already had Sophia's measure.

He discovered his father alone in the library, and as he had certain details he wished to discuss concerning the estate he managed in the north, it suited his purpose admirably to spend some time alone with the Earl.

Without any display of real warmth on either side, they greeted each other cordially enough. For his part, his lordship certainly wished it could be otherwise, that he could freely exhibit the deep affection in which he held his eldest son, but he doubted very much that Marcus would appreciate any display of emotion. And who could blame him for that? His lordship most certainly did not, for he was very well aware that if he had been more open about his disastrous first marriage, if he had not tried to spare Marcus more hurt by steadfastly refusing to tell him the truth about his mother, he himself would not have figured all these years as the villain of the piece in his son's eyes.

Well, perhaps it was too late now to attempt to set the record straight, he thought, handing his son a glass of wine, but if the opportunity ever arose in the future, he would not allow the chance to try to win his son's affection slip through his fingers. In the meantime he must be content with the respect Marcus always showed, and returned the compliment by listening intently to his son's proposed plans for the northern estate.

After nodding his head in agreement, and informing Marcus to put into effect the changes he wished to make, his lordship expected his son to bring the interview to a close. When he made no attempt to leave, and furthermore went over to the decanter to refill his glass, he knew at once that his son must have some other topic he wished to discuss, and waited patiently for him to resume his seat.

Marcus took a fortifying sip of the rich red liquid, while casting his father an uneasy glance above the rim of his glass. 'I'm no tale-bearer, sir, as I hope you know, nor am I one to interfere in something which really is none of my concern, but I think it only right that you are aware of something that happened in the park earlier, as it concerns Sophia. Or perhaps it would be more accurate to say an incident involving one of your servants.'

Marcus could see at once that he had his father's full attention. 'My friend Petersham is wishing to sell his bay, and as I'm in need of a new hack I decided to put the horse through its places. Quite by chance I came upon Sophie in a quiet area of the park. She was in the company of Sir Lucius Crawley.'

His lordship was not best pleased to learn this and wasn't slow to betray the fact. 'The devil she was!'

'She informed me that she didn't arrange to meet Crawley there,' Marcus assured him. It was not his intention to cause trouble for his sister, merely to put the Earl on his guard. 'And I believe her, sir. Sophia may have her faults, but she's certainly no liar. I honestly believe that she doesn't even like Crawley.'

The Earl grunted. 'That wasn't the impression I gained last night. The little minx danced with him twice. And I suspect it was simply because she knew I wouldn't approve.'

Marcus could not help smiling at this. His father might have turned seventy, but there was absolutely nothing lacking in his upper storey. 'I think you may possibly be right. Anyway, getting back to what I have to tell you, I arrived on the scene in time to see Crawley raise his crop to your new stable-hand, and to see the groom floor the Baronet with one flush hit to the jaw.'

'Did he, by gad!' There was more than just a hint of excitement in the Earl's grey eyes.

'Believe me, sir, I couldn't help but admire the way he did it myself. I wouldn't be at all surprised to learn that he's done some sparring in his time. There was no bluster about it. Excellent science!' The glint of admiration in Marcus's dark eyes faded. 'Still, I'm not suggesting for a moment that he should have done it, though I have to say he reacted in self-defence.'

The Earl looked across at his son steadily. 'Are you

suggesting that I should dismiss him because of the incident?'

'No, sir. I'm not.' A further wry smile tugged at the corner of his mouth. 'He may be an insolent dog, but he was only doing his duty by guarding Sophia. I understand he hasn't been with you for very long, but unless I much mistake the matter he already has my sister's measure. She would not find it easy to escape from him, and I believe he'd always guard her well.'

'I respect your judgement,' his lordship responded softly, 'and find that very reassuring to hear.' He regarded his son in silence for a moment, and noted the look of concern that remained in his eyes. 'So what precisely is troubling you, Marcus?'

'I'm not certain. I don't suppose for a moment that Crawley will bring charges of assault against the groom, not when there were witnesses to the incident, and he would probably be made to look a fool. But he's a vindictive devil…And I just didn't care for that look in his eyes before he left.'

Chapter Six

Marcus was by no means the only one to have noticed that malevolent gleam in a pair of hard, blue eyes. Benedict had not been slow to recognise that vengeful glint either and, given Sir Lucius's somewhat unsavoury character, had well expected the Baronet, at the very least, to write to the Earl of Yardley complaining bitterly, and demanding the instant dismissal of the perpetrator of the attack upon him. When, however, several days had passed and he had not even received the mildest reprimand for his behaviour in the park, Benedict began to wonder whether Sir Lucius might not be quite the black-hearted rogue he had been painted. Then something occurred to restore his former opinion of the malicious Baronet.

He had been taking one of his lordship's fine coach-horses to the blacksmith when he had first suspected that he had become the object of attention. Turning suddenly, he had caught sight of a thickset individual in a frieze coat darting down a side alley. Then, as he had sat himself down on a rough wooden bench outside the smithy, waiting for the horse to be shod, he had glimpsed the same scoundrel across the street, staring directly at the blacksmith's premises. Later that same day he had noticed him yet again loitering near the entrance to the mews; only this time he had a companion with him of equally villainous appearance.

There was little doubt in Benedict's mind that he was being watched, and his movements noted, so the following evening when Trapp, in a surprisingly sociable mood, suddenly suggested that he might like to accompany him to The Red Lion inn, and enjoy a tankard or two of ale, Benedict accepted the unexpected invitation eagerly, realising that it would offer the opportunity to confirm beyond doubt that he was, indeed, the object of someone's interest.

Dusk had almost fallen when he and Trapp left their room above the stable, but even so there remained sufficient light for Benedict to be fairly certain that there were no shadowy figures lurking in the mews. It was impossible to tell whether someone was dogging their footsteps when they turned on to the main street and walked in an easterly direction towards the tavern favoured by a great number of grooms and coach-drivers. London never slept, certainly not at this time of year, and there were just too many people abroad to be sure whether he was once again being followed.

As things turned out, it was the eagle-eyed Trapp who, once comfortably seated in the friendly inn, tankard of well-earned ale in his hand, first noticed that Benedict appeared to be the object of a certain someone's attention.

''Ere, lad,' he remarked, after swallowing a mouthful of ale and wiping his mouth on the back of his hand, 'that cove standing over there seems to be eyeing you quite a bit.' He gestured towards an ill-favoured rascal leaning against the end of the counter. 'I noticed he came in not long after us. A friend of yours, is he?'

Benedict glanced across the tap in time to see the man turn his back towards them. Even though he could not see his face clearly, he felt certain in his own mind that it was neither of the two who had been skulking at the entrance to the mews the day before, and was therefore able to say with total honesty that he'd never seen the fellow before in his life.

Trapp appeared to lose interest, and changed the subject by remarking that Lady Sophia would be requiring Ben's services again in the morning. 'That seems to have cheered you up, lad,' he remarked, noting the gleam which just for one unguarded moment flickered in his companion's eyes.

Benedict didn't attempt to deny it. 'To be honest with you, Mr Trapp. I've found it a mite wearisome these past days with so little to do. I'm a man who likes to keep himself occupied.'

The head groom found nothing amiss with this attitude. 'I know what you mean, lad. I'm of a similar bent m'self. Her ladyship gave up riding a horse a decade or more ago. His lordship will still climb into the saddle from time to time, but never when residing in town. It's only Lady Sophia that takes regular exercise. Still,' he shrugged, 'I suppose we oughtn't to complain. I can tell you now, while we remain in town, we won't get too many evenings like this one, when the family remains at home, so we'd best make the most of it.'

Benedict agreed, and in the normal course of events didn't doubt for a moment that he would have enjoyed this novel experience, for never before could he recall ever having spent an evening in a common tavern, supping ale, with only a groom for company. His pleasure in the occasion, however, was totally marred by the presence of the man leaning against the counter, who, he had noted by this time, had already glanced in his direction on several occasions.

There wasn't a doubt in his mind now that he was certainly the object of someone's interest. The question was whose? Who would interest himself in the movements of a common groom? It was not beyond the realms of possibility of course that, while he had been out and about exercising one of the Earl of Yardley's fine horses, someone from his past, a friend perhaps, had penetrated his disguise. Surely, though, if that were the case, it would be a simple matter for this friend to approach him directly. Why have him watched? he asked himself, peering down at his tankard before fortifying himself from its contents. No, there was more to it than that, instinct told him, something distinctly sinister.

'Of course, when we return to Jaffrey House we'll be kept busy enough,' Trapp continued, and Benedict, thrusting aside his disturbing thoughts, paid him the compliment of listening. 'The boys will be home from school in the summer. Then we'll certainly have our hands full! The stables is a favourite haunt of theirs.'

Benedict had gained the distinct impression from their conversation a few days before that Sophia was very fond of her twin younger brothers, and he himself was very much looking forward to making their acquaintance. The meeting, however, would not take place whilst he was still in the guise of a groom, if he could possibly avoid it. It was bad enough having been brought into contact with the eldest brother. Lord Angmering was no fool, and Benedict didn't doubt for a moment that Marcus would have little difficulty in recognising the Duke of Sharnbrook when they met in the not too distant future. He would need to cross that bridge when he came to it. In the meantime he had more than enough to concern him.

Once again he found himself glancing across at the counter in time to catch a pair of decidedly unfriendly eyes staring fixedly back across at him. Surly and unkempt, the rogue bore all the appearance of someone who would do virtually anything for money, perhaps even murder. But who on earth disliked him so much, bore him such a grudge, that he was prepared to hire ruffians in order, perhaps, to attain his ends? He smiled grimly as one name, and one name only, sprang to mind.

If his suspicions were correct, and Sir Lucius Crawley had hired a pack of ruffians to satisfy his lust for revenge, then Benedict did not want Trapp involved in the inevitable confrontation. He had quickly come to respect this frequently gruff, hard-working man, and although he didn't doubt for a moment that he would give a good account of himself if set upon, Benedict had no intention of allowing this to happen if he could possibly avoid it.

So, after tossing the remaining ale down his throat, he carried the empty tankards across to the counter. Trapp glanced up, surprised, when Benedict returned, setting just the one refilled vessel down on their table, and then did not offer to resume his seat.

'What's this then? Ain't you joining me, lad?' he asked, not attempting to conceal his disappointment.

'No, Mr Trapp. One is more than enough for me,' he lied. It was the best home-brewed he'd tasted in many a long year, and in normal circumstance he would have been quite content to have remained all evening. 'I'll get back and check on the horses. You stay here and enjoy your ale.'

Trapp did not attempt to argue and, being unsociable by nature, would have been more than happy to sit by himself supping his ale had he not happened to notice the rat-eyed rogue who had been propping up the counter follow Ben from the inn.

He had no reason to suppose for a moment that Ben had lied, that he did, in fact, know the man, and he began to feel decidedly uneasy. Some sixth sense warned him that all was not as it should be. He just hadn't liked the look of that fellow—a villain if ever there was one!—and it seemed just too much of a coincidence that he should have chosen to leave when young Ben had.

Abandoning his tankard, he wasted no time in following. Fortunately Ben had chosen to take the same route back to the stables by which they had come, and Trapp quickly caught sight of his tall, long-striding figure some distance ahead. Unfortunately he could also see the stranger following, and closing fast.

He increased his own pace, and was certainly gaining on his quarry, when what he had feared happened: two men suddenly appeared from nowhere and, aided and abetted by the stalker, hauled Ben into a side alley. The street was busy, crowded with carriages, but there were very few people about on foot and, seemingly, no one except himself had seen the incident, or if someone else had, he or she was disinclined to become involved.

Galvanised, Trapp ran with surprising speed for a man who would not see fifty again, and arrived at the entrance to the narrow alley in time to witness Ben, still manfully attempting to grapple with the three stocky attackers, suddenly tumble to the ground.

Slightly stunned by the heavy fall, Benedict was forced to sustain a volley of merciless kicks and blows before one of the attackers was blessedly hauled from the fray. Out of his rapidly swelling left eye he caught sight of his valiant rescuer delivering a punishing blow to the villain who had followed him from the inn and, summoning up his last reserves of strength, took immediate action by smashing a size-able stone against a well-muscled leg. The assailant fell back, groaning in agony, too badly injured to be a further threat.

Marcus had been correct when he had supposed that his father's newest employee had sparred in his time. Benedict was indeed a keen exponent of the art, and he had little difficulty in dealing effectively with the third and last assailant. Quickly scrambling to his feet, he delivered one powerful blow which sent the man in the frieze coat sprawling to the ground, and a merciless clasp on a grubby neckcloth kept him there, gasping for air.

'Who paid you to kill me?' Benedict hissed, piti-lessly maintaining his constricting hold.

'Not kill,' the man croaked, ineffectually clawing at the powerful fingers while fighting for breath. 'Only—only rough you up a bit.'

'Who was it?'

'Swear I don't know, guv'nor. Never seen 'im afore. Came in The Three Ferrets a day or so back looking for someone who'd do a job for 'im.'

It would have afforded Benedict supreme satisfac-tion to squeeze the very life out of the rogue, but sense prevailed, and he released his hold. 'Describe him! What did he look like?'

'A weedy cove in black clothes.'

This was hardly a description of Sir Lucius, but then, Benedict reminded himself, Crawley was unlikely to have gone about hiring thugs himself. 'A servant?'

'Aye. Looked like it to me.' The hired thug raised a hand to his throat, but wisely refrained from attempting to escape. 'Told me where to find you, told me what you looked like too. Wanted you followed, see? Then, when the time were right, we were to give you a good 'iding. But we weren't to take our time about it, not if we wanted the rest of the money. The cove wanted the job done quick, like.'

With lips bruised and bleeding, Benedict managed a twisted smile as he hauled his captive to his feet by the lapels of the worn frieze coat. 'Well, it would seem you've earned your full reward, you rogue.'

'Eh?' The man looked bewildered, suspicious and hopeful in equal measures. 'Ain't yer going to turn us over to the Runners?'

Benedict didn't answer, but glanced up the deserted alley. Some detached part of his brain had registered that the man with the injured knee had limped away long since, quickly followed by the second partner-in-crime, with the doggedly determined Trapp hard on their heels.

'If I did that then you'd be quite unable to collect the remainder of your ill-gotten gains, now, wouldn't you?' he responded at last. 'Not that I think you'll have an easy time of collecting your—er—blood money.'

'No 'ard feelings, guv'nor, eh?' The small but sturdy villain looked even more unprepossessing when he smiled. He had several teeth missing, undoubtedly the result of his nefarious activities, and what few remained were black and decayed. 'These be 'ard times, and work be 'ard to come by. A man must take what 'e can get.'

'Work?' Benedict echoed, totally unmoved. 'Yes, and there are those who aren't too particular what they do so long as they get their reward. Which brings me back quite nicely to what I was saying earlier…Are you quite certain that you shall receive your dues?'

It was quite obvious from his expression that the villain wasn't at all sure. 'Told me he'd be in The Three Ferrets the day after tomorrow. And he'd better be there!'

'Take it from me, he won't be,' Benedict assured him with a certain grim satisfaction. 'But you will be paid in full if you do precisely what I tell you…'

The following morning Sophia left the house just before noon. Since the unfortunate encounter with Sir Lucius Crawley she had made a point of never taking exercise at the same time each day, in the hope that in this way she could avoid any further confrontations with would-be suitors. Her brother's escort, of course, had ensured that there had been no repetition of the unfortunate incident in Hyde Park, and she had very much enjoyed having Marcus with her for the past few days, for he could be the most amusing companion when he set his mind to it. Nevertheless she couldn't deny that she was very much looking forward to furthering her acquaintance with her enigmatic groom.

Consequently she was most disappointed to see her father's trusty henchman awaiting her arrival outside the house, and demanded to know why Ben was not to escort her.

If Trapp felt aggrieved by this total lack of enthusiasm for his company, he certainly betrayed no sign of it. 'Had a bit of a mishap, as yer might say, m'lady, and so I've relieved 'im of his dooties.'

Sophia was not slow to notice that the head groom himself was sporting a fine black eye. 'You also appear to have sustained an injury yourself, Trapp. What on earth has been happening? You look as if you've been in a mill.'

'A mill, m'lady?' he echoed, trying to appear the picture of innocence. 'Now, what on earth makes you suppose that I'd indulge in a bout of fisticuffs? I'm a peaceable man, I am.'

Raising a decidedly sceptical brow, Sophia allowed him to help her into the saddle. 'No one would think you peaceable, Trapp, if they'd ever heard you rant and rage at the stable-boys back at Jaffrey House.' She didn't quite catch his muttered response, but didn't trouble to ask him to repeat himself, and merely demanded to know what, precisely, had occurred to render Ben incapable of escorting her out that morning.

'Oh, he were more than ready to do so, m'lady, but I thought he ought to rest.'

Sophia succeeded in maintaining her temper, but it was an effort. 'And still I'm waiting for an answer, Trapp. No doubt you'll oblige me in your own good time.'

The sarcasm was not wasted on him, and he could not forebear a smile. His master's only daughter always put him in mind of a little terrier dog—inquisitive and determined, never willing to release its hold once it had its teeth into something.

'Titus decided to take exception to a rat visiting his stall, and lashed out. Unfortunately young Ben just 'appened to be standing behind him at the time and copped the hoof full in the chest, poor lad!'

As Titus, the most placid of all her father's fine carriage horses, had never been known so much as to draw his ears back when pestered by a yapping dog, Sophia found this explanation very hard to believe. 'And I suppose Ben caught you in the eye with his elbow while he was reeling from the impact.'

'Aye, that's the way of it, my lady,' Trapp confirmed, the derisive note in her voice having gone completely undetected this time, and Sophia, faintly smiling, decided to say no more for the present, thereby successfully lulling her father's minion into a false sense of security.

She maintained quite beautifully an air of sublime unconcern, not once attempting to raise the subject again, not even to enquire into the extent of her personal groom's injuries. After a sedately ridden circuit of the park, during which she stopped from time to time to exchange a few words with several acquaintances, including Lady Elizabeth and Robina, she returned to Berkeley Square and, still maintaining the innocently complaisant air, accompanied the groom round to the mews.

'I could quite easily have led your horse, my lady,' Trapp informed her while helping her to dismount.

'I know you could easily have done so,' she responded, smiling with deceptive sweetness, the period of feigned docility having well and truly come to an end. 'What you seem quite incapable of doing, however, is satisfying my curiosity over precisely why Ben was unable to accompany me today,' and before he could do or say anything to deter her, she was already halfway up the staircase leading to the room above the stables.

She discovered Ben lying down on his narrow bed, which seemed totally inadequate for a man of his size, browsing through an old edition of the *Morning Post*. The fact that he could evidently read never occurred to her as being in any way out of the ordinary, for she had come to the conclusion days before that she had acquired a personal groom with quite exceptional talents.

Benedict was very well aware that someone had entered. Quite naturally assuming it was Trapp, he made no attempt to rise, nor did he attempt to speak either, for although Trapp was becoming less taciturn with each passing day, there were still lengthy periods when he made not the least attempt to converse. It was only when Benedict detected the unmistakable foreign aroma of feminine perfume in the room that he troubled to lower the printed sheets in his hands, and glance round.

'My lady!' The joy at seeing her so unexpectedly induced him momentarily to forget his hurts. He tried to stand and received a painful reminder when several ribs groaned in protest.

Sophia was beside him in an instant, hand gently placed on one broad shoulder for a moment or two, urging him to remain seated. She could see clearly enough the evidence that he had been in a fight: the gash above the left eye, the cut and swollen bottom lip and the grazed knuckles.

She did not suppose for a moment that the head groom had been responsible for inflicting these injuries. Trapp, she knew, could be difficult on occasions, hard to please. Nevertheless she had never known him resort to physical violence before in order to maintain his high standards, except on one or two occasions when he had been caught administering a sound box round the ear to a certain work-shy stable-boy back at Jaffrey House. Ben, however, was no idle lad. With his superior height and strength, not to mention the added advantage of age, he could overpower Trapp in a trice.

'What happened to you?' Gentle yet determined, she was intent on knowing the truth. 'And please do not insult my intelligence by repeating that farrago of nonsense concerning Titus.'

What in heaven's name had the inventive Trapp been telling her? Benedict wondered, detecting the sound of a heavy tread on the stairs, and wishing fervently that the crowned head of the stables would hurry and offer some guidance on how to proceed.

When they had eventually returned to their room the previous evening, and Mr Trapp, his work-roughened hands surprisingly gentle, had tended to both their hurts, Benedict had not hesitated in confiding in the man who had so gallantly come to his aid. The name Sir Lucius Crawley had meant nothing to Trapp, and although he had voiced in no uncertain terms his wish to see the vindictive Baronet receive his just desserts, he had agreed wholeheartedly with Benedict's dictum that the fewer people who knew about the incident, the better. In return Benedict had reluctantly agreed that he ought to remain out of sight as much as possible, at least until the evidence of the confrontation had begun to fade. Their carefully considered stratagems, however, had been made without taking into account the unpredictable behaviour of the very determined daughter of the house.

'I'm waiting for an explanation,' the subject of his thoughts announced, tapping her crop impatiently against the folds of her skirt, and Benedict wasn't certain whether he wished to kiss her or shake her, or both.

Trapp's eventual arrival was of little help either. In response to Benedict's enquiring glance, he merely raised his hands in a helpless gesture, proof enough that he had had little experience in dealing with unruly females, at least the two-legged kind. So Benedict had little choice but to take command of the situation, and swiftly came to the conclusion that, all things considered, only honesty would serve.

With considerable discomfort he rose to his feet, the better to face her. 'It pains me to tell you, in more ways than one, that both Mr Trapp and I were involved in a fight last night.'

'That much is abundantly obvious,' she responded, not in the least amused by his obvious attempt to make light of it all, and Trapp, feeling that it behoved him to say something, experienced a sudden flash of inspiration.

'Set upon by three ruffians. After our purses, they were. They didn't get 'em though, 'cause young Ben 'ere and me, we gave a good account of ourselves, and soon had 'em scurrying away like whipped pups.'

Ben's expression of comical dismay only succeeded in increasing Sophia's scepticism. 'Although one must deplore such behaviour, one cannot help but feel a degree of sympathy for those ruffians' plight,

Trapp,' she remarked, her tone as dry as kindling. 'They must have been desperate men indeed to have chosen you two as their victims…Desperate, or just plain stupid! Had they succeeded in their aim, they would have been woefully disappointed with their ill-gotten gains. After all, two grooms out enjoying an evening tipple hardly present rich pickings.'

Trapp looked helplessly across at his subordinate. If it was guidance he sought, then none was forth-coming, for Benedict was staring directly at Sophia, his eyes alight with amusement, and more than just a hint of admiration too.

'What really induced those men to set upon you?' she asked, directing the question at him.

'The inducement was money, my lady,' he assured her. 'They were paid to do so.'

'But why? Does someone bear you a grudge?' She found this difficult to believe, and would have dis-missed it in a trice if he hadn't appeared quite so sincere as he nodded his head. 'I would be the first to admit that I do not know you very well, but I wouldn't have supposed for a moment that you were the kind of man to go out of his way to make enemies. Do you know who instigated the attack upon you?'

He did not attempt to answer.

'Whoever hired those men must surely have pos-sessed sufficient funds to do so,' she persisted. 'Have you truly no idea who it might have been?'

Again he did not answer, but suddenly there was no need for him to do so, for all at once she realised who it must have been, and was assailed by a veritable torrent of conflicting emotions. Foremost among them was a searing sense of shame, knowing that but for her none of this would have happened, realising that her childish behaviour in trying to thwart her father's plans to marry her to some eligible *parti* had resulted in an innocent man becoming hurt.

'Crawley,' she muttered, anger coming to the fore. 'It must have been he. Rot his black heart!'

'I dare say in time he will go the way of all flesh,' Benedict responded with a flash of wry humour, but Sophia refused to be diverted.

'I do not believe that I can wait that long,' she announced, determination hardening her voice. 'Crawley's an utter blackguard, and I shall personally ensure that he pays dearly for what he has done to you.'

There was a moment's silence, then, 'Let be, my lady!'

It was undoubtedly a command, and one which had Trapp gaping in astonishment and Sophia regarding her suddenly authoritative groom in a mixture of anger and surprise. It was evident that she was unaccustomed to being spoken to in such a fashion, least of all by a servant. Nevertheless Benedict was not deterred.

'I do not require a female to fight my battles for me,' he went on in the same resolute tone. 'I may not, at this present moment in time, be in a position to extract due penance, but I have a long memory and shall not forget Sir Lucius Crawley's behaviour in a hurry. In the meantime it would be in our own best interests, both yours and mine, to let the matter rest.'

It was easy to detect both anger and resentment in her expression. Benedict, regarding her keenly, could discern a flicker of admiration too, and finally he detected the reluctant acceptance before Sophia swung away and walked the few paces to the head of the stairs.

'Very well, Benjamin Rudgely, it shall be as you wish,' she flung over her shoulder. Then she was gone without uttering another word, leaving Trapp gaping in utter astonishment once again.

'Well, I'll be damned!' he announced, when at last he had found his voice. 'If I hadn't witnessed it with me own eyes, I'd never 'ave believed it.' He glanced in Ben's direction, a look of dawning wonder in his eyes. 'You're a marvel, my boy! Miss Sophia's always been a headstrong chit, wanting her own way in all things, and yet she agreed to let well alone without so much as a blink.'

'Not quite, Mr Trapp,' Benedict countered. 'Unless I much mistake the matter, she didn't find the decision an easy one to make.' He smiled softly as he eased his aching body back down on the bed. 'Headstrong and spoilt she might be, but I for one do not doubt for a moment that she will keep her word.'

Chapter Seven

Benedict's faith in the young woman who had succeeded in capturing his interest like no other female had done before was not misplaced, as he discovered for himself two days later when he received an unexpected summons to present himself at the house promptly at midday.

As Trapp had driven the Earl and Countess out in the light town carriage half an hour earlier, Benedict had a fairly shrewd idea of precisely who wished to see him. Prepared though he was, he still found his pulse rate soaring when he entered the library at the appointed time to discover the raven-haired darling who continued to bewitch him seated at the mahogany desk, busily engaged in writing a letter.

Disappointingly there was no smile of welcome this time, as she instructed him to be seated in the chair on the opposite side of the desk, but Benedict refused to be too downcast. She appeared totally absorbed in the letter she was writing, so he made no attempt to interrupt her, and merely occupied himself by taking stock of the book-lined room.

Unlike Trapp, Benedict quite understandably felt not in the least out of place in the elegant surroundings. The well-stocked shelves, and the unmistakable aroma of leather and fine old brandy, put him vividly in mind of the library at Sharnbrook. He didn't doubt for a moment that during his long absence the dedicated servants had taken excellent care of the house, and its contents. No doubt most of the rooms were swathed in holland covers, and he was very much looking forward to that day when he could order their removal and take up the many duties for which he had been groomed from birth.

Drawing his mind back to the present, he glanced across the desk to discover that the being who had been instrumental in delaying his return to the ancestral pile had finished writing and was studying him rather intently.

'Your injuries appear to be healing fast,' Sophia remarked, having observed that his lips were no longer swollen, though the gash above his left eye was still very noticeable. 'I trust, in the circumstances, Trapp has not been working you too hard.'

Benedict wasn't slow to assure her that the opposite was true, and that he had been given only the lightest of tasks. 'In fact, my lady, the sooner I'm allowed to resume all my duties, the better I shall like it.'

'In that case you may accompany me out tomorrow. My brother leaves London today, so I shall require your services from now on.'

This was music to Benedict's ears. It was not that he disliked Lord Angmering; far from it, in fact. The Viscount had often paid a visit to the stables when he had called at Berkeley Square, and his frequent caustic remarks had never failed to amuse Benedict. He could not deny, though, that the Viscount's presence in the capital had succeeded in obstructing his wooing of the Earl's delightful daughter, and he couldn't in all honesty say that he was sorry to learn of Marcus's imminent departure.

'In the meantime, however, I do not think you should be in too much of a hurry to resume all your duties,' Sophia advised softly, experiencing yet again that searing stab of guilt as she detected the clear outline of the bandages beneath the rough cotton shirt. 'I do not wish to be instrumental in causing you yet more pain.'

It was a moment or two before Benedict realised that she was referring to his physical injuries, not his present emotional state, and almost sighed with relief, for he didn't doubt for a moment that his days as the Yardleys' stable-hand would be well and truly numbered if it ever became known that he had serious designs on the daughter of the house.

'You are not to blame for what occurred the other evening, my lady,' he assured her gently, but she refused to be so nobly exonerated.

'Yes, I am, Ben,' she countered. 'I'm totally to

blame. It was my foolishness in offering encouragement to a man of Crawley's stamp that resulted in your being attacked.' She couldn't prevent a wry little smile. 'You must allow me to suffer a guilty conscience, and feel thoroughly ashamed of myself. I don't suppose for a moment that, my nature being what it is, I shall suffer this lowliness of spirits for very much longer,' she said lightly, unaware herself just how much the experience had begun to change her attitude towards a great many things.

The change in her expression, however, was instantly noticeable, and there was more than a hint of resentment in the look she flashed him. 'Of course, it certainly didn't improve my state of mind when I saw Crawley yesterday evening, and was forced to keep a civil tongue in my head because of that ridiculous promise I had made to you.'

'You spoke to him?'

'Briefly, yes,' she disclosed, not finding his evident interest in the least strange. 'Thankfully, though, he never asked me to dance.' She frowned suddenly. 'Now I come to think about it, I cannot recall seeing him dance at all. He seemed rather preoccupied, and left the party early, as I recall.' This seemed to afford Ben a great deal of amusement, and she was curious to know why.

'Because, my darling girl, I strongly suspect that Crawley's preoccupation was due entirely to my little stratagem,' he admitted and, ignoring her evident surprise at the familiarity, he went on to explain the steps he had taken to attain a modest revenge.

Sophia thoroughly approved, and it went some way to lessen her lingering feelings of guilt. 'I just hope those rascals who set upon you continue to press for payment. And attain it too!'

'I suspect that he will be forced to meet their demands in the end, if only to ensure their silence. A man like Crawley might enjoy a degree of notoriety, but engaging known felons to attain his nefarious ends would not be tolerated. He would lose face, might even be branded a coward, and that spells disaster for any member of the Ton.'

As always, what he had said was no less than the truth, and Sophia couldn't help wondering from where he had acquired this extensive knowledge of her class. Curiosity got the better of her and she found herself saying, 'You never cease to surprise me, Ben. You're quite familiar with the rules laid down by polite society. How did you acquire this wisdom, I wonder? From scanning the gossip-columns in the newspapers, perhaps?'

He would have been most surprised if sooner or later she hadn't passed some remark about his ability to read and, prepared, wasn't in the least disturbed by the half-mocking enquiry. 'Mr Trapp isn't one to indulge in unnecessary small talk, as perhaps you are aware, so reading does help to pass the time.'

Sophia digested this reply in silence for a moment. It was quite the norm for higher-ranking servants to read and write, but a stable-hand was quite another matter, and yet she could not in all honesty say that she had been at all surprised to discover that Ben had acquired these skills. 'No doubt your old master insisted that you learn.'

'He most certainly did, my lady.' Again Benedict found it not in the least difficult to return that level feminine gaze, though he continued to find it most strange referring to his late father as 'the old master'. 'He believed that a man could never hope to better himself without acquiring a little education.'

'Mmm.' Sophia regarded him in silence again, not totally satisfied with the explanation, but deciding not to press for more details at the present time, and merely waved one slender hand in the general direction of the small table near the door. 'You'll find some recent copies of the *Morning Post* over there. And if you are so inclined you may cast your eyes over the shelves before you go, and borrow any book which happens to take your fancy.'

Touched by the generous offer, Benedict was in the process of voicing his grateful thanks when the door opened and the butler entered to inform his young mistress that Miss Perceval had called and was awaiting her in the drawing-room, which effectively brought the interview to an abrupt end to the intense disappointment of at least one of the room's occupants.

Assuring Ben that he might feel free to take all the time he needed to make his selection, Sophia hurriedly left the library and went across the hall. 'It quite slipped my mind that I had invited you here this morning,' she freely admitted, entering the elegantly appointed salon in time to see her friend removing a pretty powder-blue silk bonnet from her dusky locks.

Robina wasn't in the least offended, but couldn't resist saying, 'And I suppose you've also forgotten the reason why you invited me here.'

'Oh, no, I haven't forgotten that,' Sophia assured her, smiling at the half-teasing tone. 'Although, as things have turned out, you may as well have saved yourself the trouble of calling. When I issued the invitation, I expected Marcus to be here, but he has decided to leave London today. You know what a gadfly he is, Robin.' She raised her hands in a helpless gesture. 'One just never knows where he'll be from one day to the next. Unfortunately, without his assistance I really cannot demonstrate the waltz very well, unless…'

A thought suddenly occurred to her, and she turned to the butler who had entered in her wake, bearing a tray containing ratafia and a plate of sweet almond biscuits. 'Cardew, be good enough to see if Ben is still in the library, and if he is, request him to come in here.'

The butler expressed his disapproval by giving vent to a loud sniff. He objected most strongly to outside workers having free run of the house, even those who took the trouble to titivate a little before presenting themselves at the door, but knew better than to remonstrate with the master's daughter, and went away to do as he was bid.

Although Sophia had spoken of her new groom on several occasions, she had failed completely to mention how very handsome he was, and Robina found herself almost gaping when the door opened a short while later and a tall man, his golden-brown hair easily reaching the base of his neck, walked smoothly into the room. She found herself quite unable to draw her eyes away from him. It wasn't his superior height or breadth of shoulder which struck her most forcibly, but the fact that, even dressed in rough workman's clothes, he didn't look in the least out of place in the elegant surroundings.

'Ah, good!' Sophia remarked, glancing briefly at the book and papers in his hand. 'I see you've made your selection. Lay your reading matter to one side, Ben, because I need your help.'

Betraying faint surprise, he obeyed the command. 'How may I be of service, my lady?'

Although rapidly losing the last vestiges of childish immaturity, there remained an element of roguery in her nature. 'I'm certain that such an accomplished person as yourself, at some point in his life, learned to dance.'

'Dance, my lady?' he echoed, casting a wary glance across the room in Robina's direction.

'Yes, dance, Ben. You know—that silly pastime we lesser mortals engage in when we've nothing better to do with our time.'

A suppressed chuckle from behind reminded Sophia of her friend's presence, and that she was forgetting her manners. She immediately rectified this lapse on her part by formerly making the introductions, just as though Ben had been a gentleman caller to the house, and then persuaded a slightly bemused Robina to take the seat at the pianoforte.

Robina was more than willing to oblige. Nowhere near as gifted as her sister Frederica, she could none the less play very creditably when called upon to do so, though her fingers did stumble slightly when she saw Sophia quite brazenly place one masculine hand lightly on her waist, while retaining his other in her own slender fingers.

Benedict was no less surprised. Naturally he had heard of this new dance, which was rapidly gaining in popularity, but had never performed it himself before. Nevertheless he was very willing to learn, especially if it meant that he could maintain some physical contact, frustratingly slight though it might be, with the woman who he was daily becoming more convinced would make him the perfect wife.

Sophia was not as indifferent to that light masculine touch as she tried to appear, either. She recalled clearly that evening at Christmas when Marcus, after a little persuasion, had taken the trouble to teach her the dance which was still considered by many to be extremely improper, but she couldn't recall feeling in the least conscious of her brother's touch when he had swirled her round the drawing-room at Jaffrey

House, and it took a monumental effort on her part to marshal her thoughts and concentrate on the task in hand.

She swiftly discovered that either she was an excellent teacher, or Ben was a remarkably apt pupil. After one or two minor lapses in concentration, when they neatly avoided stepping on each other's toes, they were soon swirling about the large drawing-room in perfect harmony, until Sophia inadvertently caught the toe of her slipper under the edge of the carpet. Only her partner's lightning reflexes prevented her from falling. One strong arm snaked round her slender waist, and she was held protectively against a stone hard chest for a moment before being set gently back on her feet.

The contact was brief, moments only, and yet every inch of her body was left tingling with a wealth of sensations which brought colour rushing to her face. She instinctively took a step away, and risked a fleeting glance up at the man whose touch had wreaked such havoc with her senses, only to discover that he wasn't even looking at her, but across at the instrument in the corner of the room. It was only then that she realised that the music had stopped.

'My, my! What an energetic dance the waltz is!' she exclaimed, striving to control her erratic breathing as she followed the direction of his half-amused gaze to discover Robina, fingers poised above the keys, looking decidedly thoughtful. 'I think we'll end the first lesson there, don't you? I feel quite exhausted.'

This was no less than the truth, but it didn't account for the sudden feeling of shyness which assailed her, and she discovered that it was as much as she could do to nod dismissal to Ben, before moving across to the sofa.

Robina joined her the instant the door had closed behind him. 'You appear to have acquired a most accomplished groom.'

The quietly spoken observation in no way struck Sophia as odd. In fact, she would have been most surprised if her very observant friend had not noticed that there was something very singular about Benjamin Rudgely.

'More accomplished than you realise,' she responded, having swiftly regained much of her composure, and wondering why she had come to lose it in the first place. 'Every time I'm in his company, I learn something new about him. Why, only the other day I discovered that he can read and write.'

'Good heavens!' Robina did not attempt to hide her surprise. 'Unusual, don't you think?'

'Very,' Sophia agreed. 'But then Benjamin Rudgely is a most unusual man.'

Reaching for the ratafia, conveniently placed on the nearby table, she poured out two glasses, handing one to Robina before leaning back against the sofa to sip hers meditatively. 'It wouldn't surprise me to discover that he was some rich man's by-blow.'

A vicar's daughter she may have been, but Robina was neither naïve nor easily shocked. She merely gazed at some distant spot, as though conjuring up a vision of a handsome face with undeniably aristocratic features, and after a moment or two nodded in agreement.

'He always refers to his late employer as "the old master",' Sophia explained. 'I have a strong feeling, though, that the relationship between them was rather more than that of master and servant. After all, how many people would take the trouble to ensure that their servants received an education? I know my father did just that with Trapp, but it is unusual, you must admit.'

Again her friend nodded in agreement. 'So you think that his old employer might well have been his father?'

'It's a possibility, certainly.'

'But you don't know his name?'

'No, I don't,' Sophia freely admitted. 'Furthermore, I have no intention of trying to discover it, either. If Ben wishes me to know, he'll tell me—if not, then I'm certain he has his reasons for not doing so.'

Robina's regard turned from merely interested to downright penetrating in a matter of seconds. 'You have evidently taken a keen interest in your groom, Sophia,' she remarked softly.

'Yes, I suppose I have.'

'You have grown fond of him, I think.'

'Yes,' she admitted, seeing no earthly reason to lie. 'But I was also very fond of Clem, remember?'

'Yes you were…But Clem, let me remind you, was

short, slightly on the portly side, and certainly no Adonis, whereas Benjamin Rudgely…'

'Is excessively handsome,' Sophia finished for her, for the first time hearing a tiny alarm bell ringing, but steadfastly refusing to heed its warning. 'Yes, I had noticed that myself, Robin. I'm not blind. But if you are trying to imply that there is anything improper going on between—'

'I'm not suggesting anything of the sort,' Robina hurriedly assured her. 'It's just that…' there was more than a flicker of concern in her soft blue eyes '…you have never been one to hide your feelings. Everybody knew how fond you were of your old groom, and no one living in the four Abbey villages thought anything of that friendship. But this is London, Sophia, a veritable hotbed of scandal and malicious gossip. If you display the same affection for this new groom as you did for Clem, then I dread to think of the vicious rumours which might begin to circulate.'

Sophia sat silently digesting what Robina had said for a few moments, then, reaching for a sweet almond biscuit, gave a tiny dismissive wave of her hand. Her friend was making far too much of it!

As things turned out, Robina's fears were well-founded. Before too many days had passed, Sophia and her handsome groom had become a regular sight in the park, and gossip and speculation had not been slow to follow. A great many people, of course, saw nothing amiss in a young lady and her groom riding side by side, deep in conversation; while others, most especially those who had attended the Yardley ball the previous month, could not help wondering if there might be some truth in the gossip which had been circulating at the time. After all, Lady Sophia Cleeve had paid precious little attention to any gentleman of the Ton since her arrival in town, and yet here she was quite brazenly displaying the keenest interest in a lowly groom!

Sophia remained oblivious to the many surreptitious winks and malicious whispers exchanged behind her back. She was conscious only of the fact that London had become excessively crowded, its population seeming to have doubled overnight. No matter what time she chose to take her daily ride, it was impossible to find a street that was not teeming with traffic, or a spot in the park that was not peppered with gossiping couples, a circumstance that prompted her to complain bitterly to her parents at the breakfast table one morning, a little over a week after Marcus's departure from town.

The Countess cast her daughter an understanding smile. 'I'm afraid, my dear, you must grow accustomed to it. The Season has begun, and the majority will remain until its conclusion.'

'I realise that, Mama, but it seems to me that everyone has descended on the capital during the past few days.' She was struck by a wicked possibility. 'In fact, to be precise, the influx has occurred since Marcus's departure. Perhaps we ought to summon him back, and see if his presence cannot induce some to return to their estates.'

His lordship, absently browsing through the pile of correspondence by his plate, found himself quite unable to suppress a chuckle at this impish sally. 'Anyone listening to you, my girl, might be forgiven for supposing that you hold your brother in very low esteem, whereas in fact the opposite is—'

He broke off, his face turning such a sickly hue that the Countess was prompted to ask if he were feeling quite the thing.

'W-what…?' He gazed wide-eyed across the table at her, just as though she were a complete stranger. Then he seemed to collect himself and hurriedly rose to his feet, gathering together all his correspondence as he did so. 'I'm fine, dear…Yes, I'm fine. If you'll excuse me, I shall finish reading these in the library.'

'I do hope he hasn't received bad news,' Sophia remarked the instant he had left them.

'Something certainly seems to have disturbed him,' the Countess was forced to concede, but flatly refused to speculate on what might have caused her husband's momentary distress, and promptly changed the subject by voicing the hope that her daughter's letter did not contain bad tidings.

'Quite the contrary,' Sophia assured her. 'It's from Olivia Roade Burton. I wrote to her last week, but it would appear she hasn't received my letter as yet, for she writes that she considers me the biggest beast in nature for having forgotten her so quickly.'

'That young lady,' her ladyship responded, her tone suddenly clipped, 'has no right to criticise anyone, not after the way she behaved.'

Sophia could not help smiling at this rare display of staunch disapproval on her mother's part. 'I am well aware that you do not think too highly of Olivia, Mama. Perhaps she is a trifle selfish and spoiled. But then so am I.'

'Very true, my dear,' her ladyship agreed, not attempting to spare her daughter's feelings. 'I am persuaded, however, that you would never play fast and loose with a gentleman's feelings by promising to marry him in one breath, then changing your mind in the next. And before you come to Miss Roade Burton's defence,' she went on, interrupting her daughter's attempt to do just that, 'I shall tell you plainly that I never for one moment believed that farrago of nonsense dear Lord Ravensden put about, suggesting that they had never been officially engaged and that the announcement which appeared in the newspaper had been a dreadful mistake.'

What her mother had said happened to be no less than the truth, and Sophia felt it would be quite useless attempting to show her friend Olivia in a more favourable light by suggesting that the events which had taken place several months before had been quite otherwise. So she merely said, 'A gentleman to the last, then, Mama! That is perhaps why you like Lord Ravensden so much, and why you were so very glad when he decided to marry Beatrice. You have always much preferred Beatrice to her sister…Come, confess it!'

The Countess, truthful to the last, never attempted a denial. 'And I, for one, feel that Ravensden had a lucky escape when Olivia took it into her head to jilt him.'

'You are perfectly right,' Sophia agreed. 'I might not approve Olivia's methods, but the outcome of her actions was to the benefit of all concerned. Furthermore,' she added, with a little knowing smile, 'I do not truly believe you blame Olivia for refusing to marry a man who did not love her.'

'Perhaps not, dear,' her ladyship answered, but flatly refused to concede more than this, and changed the subject by asking if the letter contained any interesting gossip.

'Not very much, no.' Sophia quickly scanned the single sheet. 'She mentions that the Abbey villages seem deserted. Which is hardly surprising since I swear that most of the inhabitants have descended on the capital. I'm certain I spied Beatrice herself driving out with Ravensden yesterday, and I feel sure I saw Lord Isham, looking as grim as a thundercloud, riding in the park the other day, though I cannot say that I noticed whether or not India was with him. And, of course, you know yourself that the Percevals have at last arrived in town.'

'Yes, I did.' Her ladyship found herself quite unable to suppress a smile. 'From what dear Hugo was saying the other day, it would seem his mama is not best pleased with me for holding your ball before she and Hester had arrived in town. He, the darling boy, fully understood my reasons for having done so. With the hectic social calendar it would have been quite hopeless trying to squeeze in our little event once the Season had officially got under way. Which reminds me,' she went on, after fortifying herself from the contents of her coffee cup. 'You haven't forgotten that dear Hugo is to escort us to Lady Sefton's soirée next week?'

'No, I hadn't forgotten,' Sophia assured her, smiling at her mother's habit of always adding a mild endearment when mentioning the name of someone she particularly liked.

'I cannot help wondering, Mama,' an imp of mischief prompted her to add, 'why you have never attempted to promote a match between *dear* Hugo and myself, as you quite evidently hold him in such high esteem.'

Her ladyship's eyes began to twinkle. 'It is for precisely that reason that I have never done so, child. I should never dream of foisting such a mischievous little minx on the dear boy. You would never give him a moment's peace, and he is far too much of a gentleman to deal with you as you so frequently deserve.'

Sophia could not help laughing at this candid, though unflattering, assessment of her character. 'Yes, you may possibly be right. Hugo's brother would be a far better choice.'

'On the contrary, he most certainly would not!' Her
ladyship countered, shuddering at the mere thought.
'Lowell's as harum-scarum as you are, besides being
far, far too young. Oh, no, my dear. You must marry
a man whose views you respect and whose decisions
you'll accept without question. And I assure you that
if and when I meet such a person, I shall do everything within my power to promote a match between
you.'

Sophia fixed her attention on an imaginary spot on
the opposite wall as, unbidden, a vision of a tall man
with long golden-brown hair and intelligent blue eyes
sprang before her mind's eye. Ben had never been
slow to issue a mild reproof if she ever uttered something unladylike whenever they had ridden out together, and not once had she come remotely close to
bridling at his mild strictures. How very strange that
was!

Suddenly aware that her mother was regarding her
closely, she hurriedly rose to her feet. 'Well, no
doubt, Mama, I should be happy to marry such a man,
if ever we should meet. In the meantime, I mustn't
delay in replying to Olivia's letter.'

Completely forgetting that her father had sought
solace in the library, she entered the room to discover
him standing at the window. Staring out at the square,
his shoulders stooped, his expression grave, he looked
for the first time, Sophia thought, very much the elderly gentleman.

He appeared lost in his own private gloom, obliv-

ious to her presence, and she was just debating
whether to slip quietly away when he suddenly demanded to know what she wanted.

'I'm sorry I disturbed you, Papa.' Having rarely
been on the receiving end of his sharp tongue, she
was startled by his brusque tone, but didn't allow it
to upset her. Anyone could tell just by looking at his
haggard features that he was deeply upset over something. 'I had forgotten that you were in here. I wished
to write a letter, but I can come back later.'

'There's no need.' He merely sounded weary now,
and the customary spring was singularly lacking from
his step, too, as he moved across to the desk to pick
up a single sheet of paper and thrust it into his pocket.
'I shall be going out for a short while, so you may
stay to write your letter.'

Concerned, Sophia moved to one side to allow him
to pass and thought how grey he looked, the lines in
his face seeming far more pronounced. She recalled
that several years ago, when he had learned that one
of his sailing vessels had sunk during the passage
home from India, his face had worn just such a grave
expression for several weeks. It was not the loss of a
fine ship or its cargo which had upset him so much,
but the loss of life, and she could not help wondering
if just such a catastrophe had occurred again.

Praying that this was not the case, she seated herself at his desk and reached into the top left-hand
drawer for a sheet of paper, dislodging the lid of a
small box as she did so. In the normal course of

events she would merely have replaced the lid, but what she saw so captured her attention that she took out the box to study its contents more closely.

She vaguely recalled that Cardew had placed a package with the letters by her father's plate at the breakfast table earlier, and could not help wondering if this was what the package had contained, for she felt certain that she had never seen this pretty box before, nor its strange contents. The lock of silky black hair might well have been her father's, for Sophia was well aware that his lordship's locks had been as dusky as hers in his youth. There was not the slightest possibility, however, that the tiny ring lying beside the silken strands had ever been worn on his hand. Its setting was delicate, undoubtedly old, and had been fashioned for a finger as slender as her own.

Sophia shook her head in wonder, unable to comprehend why anyone should send such things to her father, for they were surely someone's treasured mementoes…Love tokens, perhaps…

Chapter Eight

The Earl of Yardley left London by hired carriage early the following morning, the twenty-second of April, without informing any member of his household, not even the Countess, where he was bound, or the reason behind his sudden departure. It so happened that he remained away from town one night only and appeared, if anything, more perturbed than ever on his return.

Sophia grew increasingly concerned, for as the days passed her father seemed to withdraw more and more within himself. He rarely attempted to indulge in any form of conversation when they did happen to meet, and remained for the most part alone in his library, with the door firmly locked against intruders.

As he never once attempted to offer any kind of explanation for his continuing depressed state of mind, and both Sophia and her mother were disinclined to pry, the reason behind the drastic change in him remained a complete mystery until Sophia received information from a most unexpected quarter which, although offering no explanation regarding his present mental state, at least disclosed his lordship's whereabouts during his brief absence from town.

Sitting in the sunny front parlour with her mother in readiness to receive morning callers, Sophia was surprised to see her father enter the room with a letter in his hand.

'Cardew inadvertently placed this among my correspondence,' he explained, handing her the missive, before unexpectedly seating himself on one of the spindle-legged chairs.

His actions ignited a spark of hope in Sophia, for although he didn't attempt to indulge in small talk, at least he seemed inclined to bear her and her mother company for a while, something which he had certainly avoided doing in recent days. She glanced briefly at her mother, sitting on the sofa beside her, quietly plying her needle. The Countess didn't attempt to make conversation either. So, following this example, Sophia remained silent, and turned her attention to the letter.

She recognised the handwriting at once, and knew even before she broke the seal precisely who had written. After quickly digesting its contents, her eyes became riveted to the hurriedly scrawled postscript, where her friend Olivia clearly stated that she had been astounded the previous week to see the Earl on horseback riding in the direction of Steepwood Abbey.

'Good heavens, Papa!' Sophia exclaimed, not thinking twice about voicing her own astonishment. 'What on earth prompted you to return to Jaffrey House last week?'

She realised her mistake the instant she had spoken. The Earl, his complexion acquiring an alarming purple hue, rose so abruptly that he almost sent his chair toppling to the floor. 'Where I go, and what I do, is purely my affair, Sophia!' he ground out. 'You would do better to concentrate on finding yourself a suitable husband, instead of interfering in matters that are none of your concern!'

Masterfully concealing her distress at what she considered an unwarranted outburst, the Countess reached across the sofa to grasp her daughter's hand the instant her husband had stormed from the room, slamming the door behind him with quite unnecessary violence. 'There, there, child,' she soothed. 'Do not look so injured. Your father is not himself, otherwise he would never have spoken to you in such a fashion.'

Sophia was not a female easily brought to tears, and she wasn't remotely close to weeping now, but she couldn't disguise her distress as she said, 'I know, Mama.' Her faint sigh was clearly audible too. 'It would be easier to bear if I had some idea what was causing Papa such concern. At first I thought he might have received some tragic news about one of his sailing vessels, but I don't imagine for a moment that that can be the reason for his deep depression, otherwise I'm certain he would have confided in us by now.'

Her ladyship nodded her head in agreement, at a complete loss herself to understand what had wrought this drastic change in her husband. 'I'm afraid, my dear, that your father has always been a man to keep his own counsel over many things. He is not a man, however, to brood unnecessarily, so I'm afraid that until such time that he overcomes his present melancholy state of mind, or perhaps takes us into his confidence, we must bear with his moods as best we can.'

Sighing again, Sophia reluctantly agreed. 'I sincerely trust, though, Mama, that we are not forced to bear with this situation for too much longer. The atmosphere in this house is becoming daily more strained. Why, even poor Cardew has taken to tiptoeing past the library door whenever he crosses the hall.'

The butler, not noticeably tiptoeing, entered the room just then to announce the arrival of the first callers to the house that day, and a moment later Lady Elizabeth Perceval, accompanied by her daughter, came tripping lightly into the room.

Sophia, for some reason which escaped her completely, was growing increasingly more sensitive to the moods of others these days, and sensed at once that something was troubling her friend. So, as soon as the Countess had engaged Lady Elizabeth in conversation, she drew her friend over to the window embrasure, asking outright what was wrong.

Robina couldn't forbear a smile. 'I didn't realise I was quite so transparent.' The brief attempt at a lighter mood soon over, she went on to divulge, 'There's no easy way of telling you this, Sophia, and I know you're not going to like it one little bit, but I think you ought to be aware of what a few very nasty-minded people are saying about you...about you and your new groom, that is.'

Robina was not slow to notice the slender body, clad in the pretty pale green morning dress, stiffen slightly, but didn't allow this to deter her from relating what she felt she must. 'Mother and I attended a small and rather informal party last night at the house of Lord Exmouth. He and his mother arrived in town only last week, and the Dowager, for some reason, appears to have taken quite a liking to me. She's a charming lady,' Robina continued, digressing slightly, 'certainly something of a character, full of life and not afraid to speak her mind, but she isn't in the least spiteful, and it was she who first mentioned this nasty rumour concerning you.'

'And what precisely did Lady Exmouth tell you?' Sophia prompted in an undertone, after casting her eyes briefly in her mother's direction.

There was a moment's silence, then, 'Because you have shown no preference for any particular gentleman's company since your arrival in town, there are those who are only too willing to believe that there might be some truth in the rumours that were circulating on the night of your own ball, that you do, indeed, prefer the company of a—er—rougher type of person.'

'Oh no,' Sophia murmured, the muscles in her stomach twisting themselves into painful knots of anger, and bitter regrets. For the second time in the space of two short weeks she was being made to suffer the consequences of her own folly. There was no denying the fact that she herself was wholly responsible for this current gossip. She didn't mind so much for herself, but she had no wish for the rumours to reach her dear mother's ears, especially not now.

'You are certainly not without your champions,' Robina assured her in an attempt to lessen her friend's evident distress. 'Mama dismissed the talk with an impatient wave of her hand, saying that you had been reared to show consideration to servants, no matter how lowly their place in the Earl's household.' A sudden glint in her eyes betrayed the sportive element in her nature which very few had been privileged to experience. 'And Lord Nicholas Risely was overheard to say he wasn't in the least surprised that you betray a marked partiality for your personal groom, since he happened to know for a fact that the servant was responsible for saving you from falling beneath the wheels of a carriage one morning in Bond Street.'

'Lord Nicholas said that?' A reminiscent smile curled up the corners of her mouth. 'A slight exaggeration,' she admitted, 'but I'm grateful to him, all the same.'

'To be sure, I didn't know whether to believe him or not, for I felt certain you would have told me if anything of that nature had happened to you.' That sportive gleam flickered once again. 'But that didn't prevent me from assuring any one who asked for confirmation that it was perfectly true.'

Sophia could feel the tension in her slowly ebbing. 'You're a good friend, Robin. One of the best,' she told her, bringing a rush of colour to delicate cheekbones.

Although it would have afforded her much pleasure to show her utter contempt for the gossips by ignoring the rumours about her and continuing to behave as usual, Sophia knew that for her mother's sake she could not. The Countess had done everything humanly possible to make their stay in town a happy one. Even during the past trying days, when she had been forced to contend with the Earl's almost reclusive behaviour, she had continued to be an unfailing source of comfort and support, and the least Sophia could do in return was to try to avoid causing her mother further anxiety.

So when she left the house early in the afternoon to enjoy her customary daily ride, she was determined to behave with the utmost propriety, as befitted her station in life. Unfortunately the resolve, unselfishly motivated though it was, had been made without taking into account the feelings of someone whose companionship had come to mean rather more to her than she yet realised.

The instant Benedict saw her emerge from the house, and noted the tense set of those delicate features, he suspected that something had occurred to disturb the calm waters of her mind. The faint, well-bred nod in response to his greeting succeeded in confirming this belief, and the lack of invitation to ride beside her put the suspicion that all was not as it should be beyond doubt.

Racking his brains to think of what he might have said or done to upset her, Benedict followed out of the square, keeping a discreet distance. Nothing very obvious sprang to mind. In fact, he remembered quite clearly that they had parted very amicably after their ride the previous afternoon, during which they had discussed a variety of topics ranging from the war with France to the appalling conditions endured by the London poor. So he was fairly certain that he was not responsible for her present decidedly frosty mood.

Having worked in the Earl of Yardley's stables for over a month, he had by this time acquired a fair knowledge of Sophia's character, and infatuated though he still might be, he certainly wasn't blind to her faults. She could still be disturbingly impetuous on occasions, and was frequently outspoken, but these slight flaws only seemed to enhance her charm. Added to which, it was very much to her credit that she wasn't in the least missish, nor prone to take a pet over mere trifles. He was forced to conclude, therefore, that she must have a sound reason for treating him with complete indifference.

He couldn't prevent a wry smile from curling his lips as he considered his present unenviable situation. Had he truly been a groom, born and bred to the life, he would probably have accepted his young mistress's indifference to his presence without so much as a blink. But he was Sharnbrook, with proud aristocratic blood flowing through his veins, and he'd be damned if he would tolerate being ignored by the young woman who was destined to become his Duchess!

The instant she glimpsed that tall figure looming alongside Sophia could feel the tension in her steadily mounting, but the command for him to fall back a pace which rose in her throat lacked the conviction to reach her lips. How could she now begin to treat this man like a servant when she had never done so before? Impossible to tell him to remember his station in life when she herself was finding it increasingly difficult not to think of him as an equal!

She risked a sideways glance in his direction, noted that those strikingly clear blue eyes regarding her in turn totally lacked even the smallest degree of deference, and could not help wondering if she had been slightly at fault to allow him so much licence. Yet, she reminded herself, it was quite understandable in the circumstances why she had done so.

Without having really been aware of it she had, she

supposed, instinctively turned to Ben for that wholly masculine companionship which she had enjoyed with her father over the years, but which had been denied her during recent days. It had not seemed in the least odd to do so either, for Ben was an attentive listener, and an interesting conversationalist whose frequent pithy remarks had never failed to make her laugh. Strangely enough, his views on many topics were not dissimilar to her father's, and she couldn't help thinking that if he lost that rich country burr, and was dressed appropriately, he would not seem in the least out of place at either White's or Boodle's, depending on his political views, of course. She felt certain, too, that many of the famous society hostesses would not object to his gracing their elegant drawing-rooms, either.

The thought made her chuckle, and she turned her head to discover the object of her thoughts regarding her with a faint look of surprise.

'Well, thank heavens for that!' he announced in a distinctly half-mocking tone. 'I was beginning to think you'd suffered a death in the family. Or, worse still, that I had fallen from favour.'

'Oh, no. That would never happen,' she assured him softly.

Her smile faded as they rode side by side into the overcrowded park, and she noticed a certain notorious gossip in an open carriage snickering behind her hand as she glanced in their direction. 'It's hateful tabbies like Lady Tockington, over there, who put me out of temper. Is her life so empty, so grossly uninteresting, that she can find nothing better to do than spread malicious untruths about people?'

Having always kept half an eye open for any old friends who, although not having seen him for more than five years, might quite easily penetrate his disguise, Benedict had been aware for several days that he and Sophia had been the object of no little attention, and could guess precisely what was being said about them. The best way of dealing with the situation, of course, was simply to ignore it, for sooner or later the gossips would find a new object on which to vent their spite. Unfortunately, his position was, to say the least, slightly precarious. Although he felt fairly certain that his disguise had not been penetrated thus far, he wasn't so very confident that it could withstand too close a scrutiny, and being discovered now just might result in his losing completely what he had been striving so hard to attain.

He returned his gaze to his future wife's lovely profile, slightly marred now by a very disgruntled expression. 'Perhaps it might be wise in the circumstances, my lady, to engage Mr Trapp as your escort, at least until the gossips have turned to a new source with which to ply their despicable trade,' he suggested, and was faintly surprised when she immediately nodded her head in agreement.

'Ordinarily, Ben, I wouldn't care a jot what was being said about me,' she admitted. Upset and annoyed though she was, she could not prevent a tiny rueful smile tugging at the corners of her mouth. 'The fact of the matter is I do like you, and I really do not care who knows it.'

She glanced at him then, but a little too late to see the gleam of satisfaction her admission had brought momentarily to his eyes. 'But for once, I'm not thinking of myself. My poor mother has enough to contend with at the moment without having to concern herself with nasty rumours about me.'

Sophia did notice his slightly puzzled frown, and without a second thought decided to confide in him. 'The Earl has been behaving very strangely of late. I've never known him act this way before. He's almost in an enclosed world of his own, shutting both Mama and me out. If he were ill, I could understand it, and make allowances, but I do not believe his health is the issue here.'

Although he had never had any personal dealings with the Earl, Benedict had discovered from Trapp that his lordship was in remarkably good health for a man of his advanced years. He also knew about his lordship's unexpected short absence from town the previous week, and suggested that something might have happened while the Earl had been away to cause him some concern.

Sophia considered this for a moment, then shook her head. 'I remember quite clearly that something had upset him the day before he left the capital. Besides,' she shrugged, 'I discovered only this morn-

ing that he paid a visit to our country home when he
left London.'

'And what do you suppose prompted him to visit
there?' Benedict asked, not so much interested in the
Earl's activities as concerned over Sophia's peace of
mind. She was evidently worried about her father, and
anything that troubled her was of immense impor-
tance to him now.

'He was seen riding towards Steepwood Abbey,'
she confided, 'so one can only assume that he had
every intention of visiting Sywell. But just why Papa
should suddenly take it into his head to do so, and at
such a time, remains a mystery.'

Benedict thought it rather odd too. Then memory
stirred. 'I recall your mentioning once that your father
was intent on buying the Abbey. Perhaps he had
learned that Sywell is at last considering selling the
place, and was determined to put in his bid before
any one else was given the chance. After all, Sywell
has no near relatives to whom he could bequeath the
property.'

'That isn't strictly true,' she corrected, smiling
faintly. 'There's always his Marchioness.'

Stunned, Benedict almost found himself gaping.
When on earth had Sywell taken the matrimonial
plunge? It must have been during the time that he
himself had been away in the Caribbean. However,
he was more inclined to think that his darling girl,
possessing something of a teasing nature, was hoax-
ing him.

'It's true,' she assured him, having no difficulty whatsoever in following his train of thought. 'He married his bailiff's ward, a young woman of about my own age. Young enough to be Sywell's granddaughter!'

'Good gad!' he said faintly, no longer doubting her word.

'One can only suppose that after years of producing illegitimate offspring, he felt inclined to produce a legitimate one.' She shrugged. 'Though whether he succeeded or not is anyone's guess.'

'Highly unlikely, I should say. He's left it rather late to consider producing an heir.'

'Well, I wouldn't know about such things,' she freely admitted. 'Though I dare say you might be able to enlighten me,' she added, when broad shoulders distinctly shook with suppressed laughter.

'I dare say I could, and might well do so when I consider you old enough to know about such things.'

Such familiarity was deserving of a severe reprimand, but Sophia found herself laughing, something which she had not done in several days. 'You are an impudent rogue, Benjamin Rudgely, and I really don't know why I bear with you. It will be a relief to have the respectful Trapp escorting me from now on.' But nothing could have been further from the truth, and she suspected that the tall man riding beside her knew that perfectly well.

With the possible exception of her father, there was no one whose company she preferred more than

Benjamin Rudgely's. Unlike a great many gentlemen with whom she associated during the evenings, Benedict was never dull, nor ever at a loss to introduce a new and interesting topic on which to converse, and, most important of all, he never required an explanation if she ever ventured a mild witticism or slightly provocative remark. He was quite simply exceptionally good company, and possibly one of the most interesting members of his sex she had ever met. Which made her ponder anew on why he was working in a situation that was far, far beneath his capabilities.

Casting a further sideways glance, she caught him staring about, those intelligent, clear blue eyes of his scanning the other occupants of the park in a way that was anything but respectful. Yes, she mused, there was certainly something proud in his bearing; one might even go so far as to say haughty. It was almost as if he did not consider those wealthy members of society who were now parading in their finery in any way superior to himself, and she truly felt that if he ever did manage to lose the countrified burr, and was dressed appropriately, he certainly would not seem in the least out of place in the most fashionable London salons.

She shook her head at the thought, wondering if she were not allowing her sincere regard for the man riding beside her to cloud her judgement. Yet, at the same time, although Ben had never once attempted to confide in her, she could not rid herself of the feeling that he had at some time in the not too distant past enjoyed a far more comfortable existence than he did now living with Trapp above the stables. She strongly suspected too that he had held a far more responsible position, one where he had issued the orders, not taken them. So why in heaven's name, she wondered, had he accepted work in a stable, when he was capable of doing so very much more? Was it simply that he had been unable to find a more responsible position since his return to England, or was there, perhaps, some underlying reason for his doing what he was doing now?

Benedict, turning his head suddenly, caught the pensive look, and completely misjudging the reason behind the expression, said, 'If you take my advice, my lady, you will not worry too much over your father. No one can possibly go through life without being troubled over something from time to time. The Earl, it sounds to me, is the kind of man who will confide in others only when he's ready to do so, and not before.'

And he is by no means the only one, Sophia decided, surprisingly realising that her father and the man at her side were not so very dissimilar. Which was most strange, because they could not possibly have very much in common…Or could they?

'My lady, you mentioned when first I came to work for your family that I might take some time off to visit my relatives,' he remarked, breaking into her perplexing thoughts, 'and I was wondering whether you'd permit me to pay a visit to my brother later this afternoon?'

She didn't take even a moment to consider the matter. 'Of course you may. I'm sure Trapp can manage quite well without you for an hour or so. In fact, I wish I could accompany you. The atmosphere in the house at the moment is strained to say the least.' There was an element of recklessness in her sudden laughter. 'Why, if my father's mood doesn't improve soon, I shall be very tempted to accept the very next gentleman who offers for me, if only as a means to get away from Berkeley Square!'

Benedict certainly did not find this in the least amusing, and his high intelligent forehead was noticeably marred by a deeply troubled frown as he fell back a few paces in order to allow one of her many admirers to draw alongside.

Chapter Nine

Before embarking on what he had once considered nothing more than a harmless little subterfuge, Benedict had arranged with his brother that, unless something arose urgently requiring his attention, there should be little or no contact between them.

Nicholas had wholeheartedly agreed, for there was always the chance that some observant devil seeing them together just might perceive the slight family resemblance, and even he, inveterate prankster that he was, balked at the mere thought of trying to explain to the world at large just why his estimable brother, whose return to fashionable society had been eagerly awaited for some little time, was masquerading as a common groom.

So he was a little surprised when, later that same day, the parlour door opened, and his brother unexpectedly came striding into the room. 'Good gad!' Nicholas exclaimed, abruptly losing interest in *the* novel which was causing no little sensation in fashionable circles. 'Taking something of a risk coming here, weren't you? Supposing you were seen?'

'I took the precaution of not attempting to gain admittance by way of the front entrance.' Swiftly realising that he would wait in vain for an invitation, Benedict lowered his tall frame into the chair opposite. 'It's surprising how quickly one grows accustomed to behaving like a servant. It's almost second nature to me now.'

'I'll take your word for that,' Nicholas responded, with an acute feeling of distaste, the mere thought of entering a dwelling by way of the area steps making him shudder. 'Evidently the novelty of playing the lowly groom has not diminished quite yet?'

Benedict's expression betrayed his feelings clearly enough even before he said, 'On the contrary, I'm heartily sick of it!'

Nicholas's sudden shout of laughter held an unmistakable note of triumph. 'I knew it would be only a matter of time before you lost interest in the delectable Sophia and turned your eyes in quite a different direction. Who's the filly that's taken your fancy now?'

Hardly the most flattering testament to one's constancy, Benedict decided, but he couldn't find it within himself to be in the least annoyed with his brother for thinking so poorly of him. If he were honest, he would be forced to admit that, when he had been Nicholas's age, he had been something of a feckless fribble, faithful to no female for any length of time.

Unable to suppress a self-deprecating half-smile, he gazed across the short distance which separated them. 'When I embarked on this somewhat shameful escapade—yes, I did say shameful, brother,' he reiterated, when Nicholas betrayed surprise, 'my reasons for doing so were purely selfish. I wished to know Sophia Cleeve a good deal better before committing myself to any lasting attachment. Ashamed though I am to admit to it, it is true none the less that in the past I have not infrequently fallen victim to a pretty face, and know full well that infatuation is a flame which may burn brightly for a time, but is seldom lasting.'

'And has the short period working in the Yardley stables extinguished the flame of desire altogether?' Nicholas prompted when Benedict, his expression completely unreadable now, fell silent and fixed his attention on the empty grate.

'No, it has not. If anything it burns brighter than ever…But, then, what I feel for the Earl of Yardley's only daughter has little to do with infatuation.'

He raised his eyes to meet his brother's interested gaze. 'I am very much in love with her,' he freely admitted, in a voice that, although lacking any vestige of emotion, sounded totally sincere. 'If I had searched the length and breadth of the land I do not believe I could have found a woman who would have suited me better. And I can only thank Providence for ensuring that our paths crossed that morning in Bond Street.'

Approval was the last thing Benedict had sought, for he considered that his choice of Duchess was his and his alone, and yet he found himself experiencing no little annoyance at the look of mild concern which momentarily flickered across his sibling's boyish features.

'Evidently you do not wholeheartedly approve my choice.'

'Oh, no, no! It isn't that exactly,' Nicholas hurriedly assured him, easily detecting the sudden steely element in the deep voice. 'I like Sophia. She's a grand girl—one of the best. In all the weeks I've known her, I've never once heard her utter a spiteful remark about any other young woman making her London début. What's more,' he continued, warming to the subject, 'she's the sort of girl a chap can talk to without his having to mind what he says all the time. She enjoys a good joke, and never needs things explained twice. Which is a great deal more than can be said for most of the little darlings gracing the town this Season.'

This was high praise indeed, but Benedict was not slow to notice that the faintly troubled look still lingered in young eyes. 'So you harbour slight reservations as to whether she would make a suitable Duchess, is that it?' he remarked, reading his brother's thoughts with uncanny accuracy, and Nicholas didn't attempt to deny it.

'Well, she ain't anything like our dear departed mama, now, is she?'

Reared from the cradle never to demean herself by the smallest display of emotion, their mother had been a cold, unapproachable woman. Not once, not even during his childhood, could Benedict recall receiving a loving word or gesture from his mother. It was little wonder that their father had not infrequently sought certain necessary comforts elsewhere, and Benedict, for one, had never thought any the worse of him for those frequent lapses.

'No, thank God!' he responded with feeling.

'Aye, she was an iceberg, right enough,' Nicholas was forced to concede. 'But you cannot deny, Ben, she knew her duty. She may not have been universally liked, not even by the members of her own family, but I lay a monkey that you've never heard it said that she ever behaved in a way which brought disgrace to the Risely name. Not that I think dear little Sophia would intentionally behave in a less than dignified manner,' he hurriedly continued, fearing that he had expressed himself rather badly. 'She's an earl's daughter, after all, and knows quite well how to conduct herself. The trouble is though, brother, she doesn't always behave as she ought, and she frequently utters the most outrageous things.'

Benedict didn't attempt to come to his future Duchess's defence, simply because his brother had spoken no less than the truth. 'I would be the first to admit that Sophia is not without her faults. Yes,' he agreed, 'she can be thoughtlessly impulsive on occasions. Disturbingly so!' he added, recalling clearly the little episode involving a certain unscrupulous Baronet. 'She doesn't always consider carefully before she speaks, either.' These to him were trifling flaws in what was otherwise an utterly charming character, consequently he didn't choose to dwell on them. 'You must remember, though, that she's still very young, not yet one-and-twenty, and in some ways remains her doting papa's pampered darling. But I rather think that she is slowly beginning to free herself from the last of those paternal ties, and leave her girlhood behind.'

He paused for a moment to study the filled decanters standing temptingly within easy reach on a nearby table and, suspecting that his abominably casual host would continue to forget his duties, decided to help himself to a large measure of brandy; the first he had sampled in many a long day.

'My life in recent weeks has not been without its enforced privations,' he admitted, after tossing half the contents of the glass down his throat and savouring its taste. 'Although I dare say my overall health has not suffered because of it, as I mentioned a little earlier, I shall not be sorry to return to my hitherto privileged existence.'

This was something Nicholas could quite easily understand, and he was not slow to voice his wholehearted approval. 'Well, thank the Lord for that! As far as I'm concerned the sooner you effect the transformation the better. All your new clothes have been delivered. They're upstairs in the spare bedchamber, just waiting for you. I'll ring for Figgins. He'll have you looking the part in a—'

'My purpose in coming here today was not to don my ducal robes,' Benedict interrupted, his voice soft but determined.

'Then why the deuce did you come?' Nicholas was at a complete loss to understand his brother's reasoning. 'You've just told me that Sophia is everything you could wish for in your future wife. You're quite obviously head-over-ears in love with the chit, so why continue any longer with the deception?'

A moment's silence, then, 'Because I believe there is a very real possibility that I might lose her altogether if I reveal my identity too soon.'

The deep lines which suddenly furrowed his brow were clear evidence of a troubled mind. 'I have had sufficient experience of the fair sex over the years, Nick, to be sure that Sophia Cleeve is not indifferent to me. What I am not quite so certain of at this point in time is whether her evident regard is strong enough to withstand the knowledge that the man of whom she is daily growing more fond is nothing more than a pompous inveigler whose actions during the past few weeks were motivated by pure self-interest.'

Managing a faint smile at his brother's astounded expression, Benedict tossed the remaining brandy down his throat before replenishing his glass from the slowly diminishing contents of the decanter at his elbow. He didn't doubt for a moment that Nicholas's astonishment stemmed from his inability to believe that any female in her right mind would ever consider for a moment refusing an alliance with the head of the noble Risely family. It was possibly true that most would not, but Sophia Cleeve belonged to that rare breed whose affections and loyalty could never be bought.

'Weeks ago,' he continued meditatively, 'when Sophia informed you that, in general, she preferred the companionship of servants, she wasn't being totally frivolous, you know,' he remarked, in an attempt to help Nicholas understand. 'She does feel a deal of contempt for the majority of her own kind, especially towards those who take flagrant advantage of their privileged positions to the detriment of less fortunate souls. And I cannot say I blame her for feeling as she does,' he went on as the names Crawley and Sywell, together with those of several other unsavoury characters, flashed through his mind. 'But, at the same time, I cannot help wondering, Nick, what makes me suppose that I am in any way superior to those she holds in such low esteem. After all, have I not lied and deceived, and made use of those less fortunate than myself in order to attain my selfish ends?' There was little humour in his sudden shout of laughter. 'For rank self-interest and arrant conceit Benedict Risely, Seventh Duke of Sharnbrook, would, I very much fear, feature very near the top of darling Sophia's list of contemptuous peers of the realm.'

He attempted to wash the bitter taste from his mouth with a further mouthful of amber liquid, but with little success. 'My main objective during these past weeks has been to determine whether or not the Earl of Yardley's lovely daughter would make me a suitable wife. It never once crossed my mind to wonder whether I would make her a suitable husband. She is not likely to overlook that piece of crass arrogance on my part. Nor the fact that I have continually lied to her almost from the moment we met.'

Nicholas, ever the optimist, voiced the belief that Sophia was not the kind of girl to take a pet over mere trifles, and was sure to forgive and forget once matters had been explained to her, but Benedict was not so certain.

'Perhaps,' he conceded, after a few moments intense thought. 'A great deal will depend, of course, upon choosing just the right moment to make a clean breast of everything. I can tell you now, brother, that I've been offered numerous opportunities to confide in her. Young, Sophia may be, but she's certainly no fool, and she has, unless I much mistake the matter, known from the start that I am not quite what I seem.'

'Do you mean she suspects that you're Sharnbrook?'

Troubled though he was, Benedict could not help smiling at this. 'No, she most certainly doesn't suspect that. In fact, I believe she's under the distinct impression that I'm some rich man's by-blow.'

Nicholas almost choked. 'Good gad!' he managed faintly, much to his brother's intense amusement.

'Yes, these past few weeks have certainly not lacked their lighter moments,' Benedict admitted, before the reminiscent smile faded and he became serious again. 'But time is no longer on my side. The last thing I want is for Sophia to discover my true identity from someone else. Which is not beyond the realms of possibility. Unfortunately I'm attaining a deal of unwanted attention at the moment.'

No further explanations were necessary. 'Ah, so you've heard what the tabbies have been saying about you both, have you?'

'Yes, I've heard. The gossip in itself doesn't worry me unduly, Nick, but the fact that I'm now being regarded with keen interest most certainly does. Sooner or later someone is going to recognise me.'

Nicholas nodded, for once in complete agreement. 'I saw your old friend Carstairs the other day, tooling his curricle along Piccadilly. And I know for certain that both Halstead and Melcham have arrived in town.'

It was inevitable that sooner or later certain of his very close friends would descend on the capital, but this did not stop Benedict from cursing long and fluently under his breath. 'If any one of those old reprobates catches a glimpse of me, I'm dished. Is our sister also in the capital, by any chance?'

'No, and isn't likely to be either, unless it's just for a day or two. I think I've mentioned before that dar-

ling Constance has lost her taste for town life.'
Nicholas took a moment or two to ponder over their
sister's surprising bent for country living, before
bringing his mind back to the present and discovering
that Benedict now appeared to have relapsed into a
world of his own, where he seemed quite content to
remain until he took his leave a few minutes later.

When the door had closed behind his caller
Nicholas stared across at the empty chair, which still
bore the imprint of his brother's well-muscled frame,
and wondered just why he had been honoured with
that unexpected visit.

Perhaps Benedict had simply wished to talk to
someone, he mused, share his hopes and fears for the
future. His big brother certainly hadn't come for the
express purpose of seeking consent for his choice of
Duchess. That much was certain! Benedict had made
up his mind that he wanted Sophia Cleeve, and
Nicholas didn't suppose for a moment that his brother
would care a jot if any member of the family disap-
proved of his choice. No, he reiterated silently, what
appeared to concern Benedict at the moment was that
Sophia herself might not want him. Could there truly
be any foundation for this fear?

He would have been the first to admit that, although
he had been acquainted with the Earl's daughter for
longer than his brother had, he didn't really know her
that well. True, they had danced together on numerous occasions, and had occasionally exchanged views
on the latest *on dits*, but not once, as far as he could

recall, had they ever indulged in any meaningful discussions.

Beautiful simpletons, Nicholas reminded himself, had never been very much to Benedict's taste; but there again neither had bluestockings. So he could only assume that the lovely Sophia fell somewhere between the two.

Reaching for the pile of gilt-edged cards on the nearby table, he began to study with interest those invitations he had received for that very evening. Surely his future sister-in-law would be attending one of these very fashionable gatherings? Perhaps if he succeeded in running her to earth, he might be able to uncover just what it was about her that had succeeded in capturing totally the interests of a man of Benedict's wide experience. More importantly, he just might be able to discover if there truly was any reason to suppose that the Earl's daughter would turn down the opportunity of becoming the next Duchess of Sharnbrook. If there was, he doubted there was very much he could do to alter the situation. But one never knew.

There were perhaps no more than a hundred guests present in the handsomely decorated salon. A very insignificant affair when compared to the several grand balls taking place that evening, Sophia reflected, as she moved about the room, automatically performing the steps of the dance.

Initially she had been delighted to discover that her

mother had accepted this invitation to Lady Carlisle's small, informal party; happier still when she had been informed, just before setting out, that the Earl had decided to escort them. That, of course, she reminded herself, was before she had realised that her father's decision had stemmed not from a desire to begin socialising again, but merely from a stubborn determination to keep an eye on his daughter's activities.

Irritated though she was, she couldn't help smiling to herself. It had taken no time at all to see through her father's little stratagem, so she could only wonder at herself for failing completely to notice that she had become the butt of some malicious gossip in recent days. Part of the reason, of course, was simply that whenever she was in Ben's company she became far too engrossed in what he was saying to take very much notice of anything else. Unlike now, when she was finding it increasingly difficult to concentrate on her young partner's conversation, and was very well aware of what was taking place around her. Even the sudden appearance in the room of a late arrival did not escape her notice.

Now what in the world had prompted Lord Nicholas Risely, of all people, to attend such an insignificant gathering as this one? she wondered, happy to let her mind wander again. Although he was not considered one of the richest prizes on the *Marriage Mart*, he was nevertheless judged to be extremely eligible, and consequently was invited everywhere. He was always to be seen at the most lavish events, and there were plenty of those taking place this night, so why had he chosen to grace this rather mediocre affair?

Intrigued, and with precious little else to occupy her, Sophia found herself following his progress into the room. She saw him relieve one of the waiters of a glass of champagne, before looking about him, as though searching for someone in particular. Their eyes met, and he raised his glass in a silent toast, before moving on and stopping from time to time to exchange a few words with various other guests.

It might have been her imagination, but he appeared disinclined to remain with any particular acquaintance for very long, and seemed intent on reaching the corner of the room where her own mother stood amid an animated little group.

The instant the set came to an end, Sophia wasted no time in returning to her mother's side in time to hear the Countess politely enquire whether there was any likelihood of seeing the Duke of Sharnbrook in town that Season.

'Not if the man possesses a ha'p'orth of sense,' Sophia could not resist saying, and found herself on the receiving end of an appreciative masculine stare.

'And why do you suppose my brother would be foolish to set foot in town?'

She suspected he knew the answer to that without being told, but had a mind to indulge him. 'Because the poor man won't be given a moment's peace, that's why. He'll have every matchmaking mama for miles around descending on him, vying to bring her daughter to his notice.'

The Countess's eyes gleamed every bit as brightly as her daughter's. 'Not quite every mother.'

'No, perhaps not every one,' Sophia agreed, casting her own a look of approval. 'But certainly most would be.'

Nicholas's gaze, openly assessing, went from mother to daughter. 'I assure you my brother is not faint-hearted. He's also quite accustomed to receiving a deal of attention, welcome or otherwise. I'm certain he'll show his face in town when he feels himself ready to do so.'

It was Sophia and her mother who now exchanged glances before the Countess said, 'Am I correct in assuming from what you have just said that the Duke has at last returned to our shores, and that you have had the felicity of seeing him again after your long separation?'

It was quite evident from his expression that Lord Nicholas was annoyed with himself for divulging as much as he had, but he did not foolishly attempt to deny the truth of what he had inadvertently disclosed. 'Yes, ma'am, I have seen him,' he admitted. 'It just so happens that I received a visit from him this very day. However, he doesn't wish his return to this country to become common knowledge quite yet. He requires a little time to—er—accustom himself to his new role in life.'

'Quite understandable,' the Countess responded,

before an acquaintance of long standing suddenly appeared at her side, demanding her attention, and it was left to Sophia to assure his lordship that neither she nor her mother was prone to gossiping, and that society would not hear of the Duke's return from either of them.

'That's a relief to know,' he answered, and sounded totally sincere. 'Benedict certainly needs some time to adjust.' He took a moment to finish the contents of his glass. 'He isn't the same person who went out to the West Indies five years ago.'

'In what way has he changed?' Sophia asked, more out of politeness than any real interest.

'Just about in every possible way,' he surprised her by divulging. 'Before he left England he was considered a leader of fashion.' He chuckled. 'To look at him now you'd never believe that! He doesn't seem to care a jot about his well-being either. Do you know that on his very first day back in town he went about exploring the slums?'

This succeeded in capturing Sophia's attention. 'What on earth prompted him to do that?'

He shrugged. 'Curiosity, I imagine. I remember he was utterly appalled by what he saw. Said that our slaves live in far better conditions than those poor wretched in the East End.'

'Ah, yes,' Sophia responded softly, and with more than just a hint of disapproval in her voice. 'I was forgetting you owned a plantation.'

'Wouldn't if Benedict had his way,' his lordship

disclosed, and noticed at once the change in her expression. 'My brother believes that no man has the right to own a fellow human being. He would free his slaves tomorrow, but fears the consequences of such an action. They're sitting on a powder keg out there. If he freed his slaves, it would undoubtedly lead to great unrest on the other plantations, and Benedict doesn't want that. He's a staunch supporter of the Abolitionists, and believes it's only a matter of time before there is an end to such an inhuman practice as owning slaves.'

Sophia found herself sharing Nicholas's noble brother's hopes, while at the same time remembering something her groom had said to her only the other day. 'You are too quick to condemn your own class, my lady. There are good and bad in every walk of life. You only have to open your eyes and ears to discover that for yourself.' And as usual he was right.

'I should very much like to meet your brother, Lord Nicholas. I believe we might discover we have much in common.'

A moment's silence, then: 'I think it could be arranged without too much difficulty.'

Suspecting that his lordship, for reasons best known to himself, was disposed to remaining at her side, Sophia took the opportunity to thank him for coming so gallantly to her defence by attempting to stem the foolish gossip presently circulating about her. 'I must say it comes to something when one cannot even hold a conversation with one's groom in public without some idiotic person starting silly rumours!'

'Think nothing of it, m'dear. Spoke out as much for my own amusement as anything else. Can't remember precisely what I said now, or to whom, but I do recall silencing a few viperous tongues.'

'So I've been reliably informed, and I'm grateful,' she responded, before changing the subject again by openly admitting how astonished she had been earlier to see him walk into the room.

He appeared nonplussed for a moment. 'Now why should you have been surprised, I ask myself? Did you suppose I consider myself too high in the instep to be seen at such a small party as this one?'

Sophia turned her head on one side, as though considering this. 'Now, how am I to answer that, I wonder…with candour or studied politeness?'

His shout of appreciative laughter resulted in more than one glance being slanted in their direction. 'So that's it!' he exclaimed somewhat enigmatically. 'Now I understand, and wholeheartedly approve. You'll suit very nicely, I do not doubt.' Then, suddenly seeming to collect himself, he changed the subject by enquiring whether she was still enjoying her first season in town.

'To be perfectly truthful, Lord Risely, it has lost much of its appeal of late,' she admitted, catching sight of her father emerging from the card-room. 'In fact there are times when I feel like suggesting an

early return to Northamptonshire,' she disclosed, and
did not notice the very troubled look which for one
unguarded moment suddenly took possession of his
lordship's handsome features.

Chapter Ten

Raising her head to glance out of the parlour window, the Countess just happened to catch sight of her daughter returning to the house. No violent slamming of the front door immediately followed her entry. Which was a great pity in the circumstances, she decided. Although in general no advocate of childish displays of temper, she couldn't help feeling that her daughter might benefit from venting any frustrations she might possibly be experiencing at the moment out on something or, better still, on someone—ideally the person solely responsible for the very unpleasant atmosphere pervading the house these days!

Returning her attention to her sewing, she began absently to ply the needle while her mind commenced to dwell, as it so often did of late, on her husband's uncharacteristic behaviour. Fanciful though it might be, she was none the less beginning to feel increasingly that she was married to a complete stranger. Gone was the kind and tolerant man whom she had known for a score of years and more, and in his place was an ill-tempered bore who appeared to delight in making himself as disagreeable as possible for much of the time.

Unable to suppress a wry smile, the Countess recalled clearly the delight she had experienced a few days before when the Earl had unexpectedly announced his intention of attending Lady Carlisle's informal party. Foolishly, as things had turned out, she had supposed that at long last he was beginning to recover from whatever it was that had caused him such distress, and that he was now, once again, ready to enjoy the numerous pleasures London had to offer. Thankfully she had not foolishly deluded herself for very long. Even before they had left the party that night, she had come to the conclusion that her husband's only reason for putting an end to the period of self-imposed isolation was simply that he had every intention of ensuring that his daughter returned to Northamptonshire at the end of the season betrothed. And unless she was very much mistaken, she suspected that their daughter was very well aware of this too!

Poor Sophia! Her ladyship experienced a surge of sympathy. The dear child must surely feel that her life was not her own any more, with her father demanding to know where she was going every hour of the day, and with whom. The evenings were worse, of course, when he made not the slightest attempt to hide the fact that he was watching her every move.

He was never slow to take her roundly to task if she stood up more than once with any gentleman whom he considered unworthy of attention. And woe betide the poor child if she refused to stand up with a gentleman whom he considered was worthy!

Her ladyship could only silently applaud her daughter's forbearance, for not once had Sophia attempted to remonstrate with her father for his unreasonable, not to say eccentric, behaviour of late. Which was a most strange circumstance in itself, she decided, after giving the matter a moment's consideration. Sophia's temperament could never have been described as placid. Even as a child she could be roused to anger with little difficulty, and had never been afraid to speak her mind. Yet not once, the Countess reminded herself, had her daughter displayed the least sign of losing her composure, handling herself with praiseworthy self-control whenever in her father's presence.

She shook her head, wondering why it had taken her until now to appreciate these subtle yet definite changes in her daughter's character which had undoubtedly taken place since their arrival in town. She didn't suppose for a moment that it was she herself who had succeeded in influencing Sophia's behaviour. Yet, someone, somewhere, was most definitely having a highly beneficial effect on the girl, changing her from an occasionally unruly and thoughtless child into a poised and gracious young woman, the

Countess decided, wondering who on earth it could possibly be.

The parlour door opened and the object of her ladyship's silent approval entered the room. Sophia had changed her habit for a simple muslin day dress and looked, if not precisely glowing with happiness, contented enough, as she seated herself at the other end of the sofa.

'Did you enjoy your ride?' she enquired, and was surprised to see a look of comical dismay bent in her direction.

'To be perfectly truthful, Mama, no, I did not. I cannot in all honesty say that I've ever found Trapp's company particularly stimulating. And it seems to me that the older he's getting the more taciturn he becomes. Or maybe,' she added, generously giving the loyal retainer the benefit of the doubt 'he isn't changing at all, and it's just that I've grown accustomed to a more stimulating companion of late.'

'By that, I assume you're referring to Clem's replacement.' Focusing her attention on her embroidery, the Countess didn't notice a faintly wary look flit over her daughter's delicate features. 'I haven't once heard you complain about him, so I assume he meets with your approval?'

'I have no fault to find with him whatsoever.'

'That is a relief to hear. I must say I had my doubts that you would ever find anyone whom you could grow to like half so well as Clem.'

'Oh, yes, Mama, I certainly…like him. I like Ben very well.'

Her ladyship noted the slight hesitation, but chose not to remark upon it and merely said, 'I cannot recall that I've ever spoken to him, apart from acknowledging his presence on the rare occasion he has been called upon to tool the town carriage, that is. Do you think he's content working for the family, or do you suspect that he might seek employment elsewhere once the Season is over? After all, residing in the country is not to every person's taste. He might prefer to remain in town.'

Receiving no response to this, her ladyship raised her eyes and was not slow to note the sudden disappearance of her daughter's normally healthy bloom. 'Why, my dear! Are you feeling quite the thing? You look as if you've just received the most severe shock.'

The laughing denial that anything was wrong sounded false even to Sophia's own ears. The fact of the matter was she felt as if she had just received a punishing blow to the pit of her stomach, and for the first time in her life experienced blind panic. If the mere suggestion that Ben might take it into his head to move on to pastures new was sufficient to make her feel physically sick, how would she feel if the suggestion became a reality?

Conscious of her mother's intense scrutiny, she turned her head to stare out of the window, lest her expression betray something that, as yet, she was not prepared to admit even to herself.

'Great heavens!' she exclaimed, relieved to be granted a legitimate reason for changing the subject abruptly. 'Lord Nicholas Risely has just entered the square…And, yes, I do believe he is heading this way! Now why, I wonder, are we being honoured with a visit from him?'

This was precisely what was passing through the Countess's mind, though she was careful not to betray the fact, when the butler showed the charmingly irresponsible young lord into the sunny front parlour a minute or so later. Although he had never failed to request Sophia to stand up with him if they happened to be attending the same function during an evening, her ladyship had never looked upon him as a serious contender for her daughter's hand, and she doubted very much that he wished to be considered a suitable *parti* by paying this unexpected visit now.

'What a very pleasant surprise, Lord Nicholas,' she greeted him, before bidding him to be seated. 'I do not believe I have seen you since our paths crossed the other evening at Lady Carlisle's party.'

'No, ma'am, you haven't. I've been out of town for the past few days, visiting a good friend of mine, Toby Alderman. He's—er—rusticating at the moment, as you might say.'

'His pockets are to let, you mean,' Sophia put in, clearly betraying the fact that, although she was increasingly growing more dignified, she still was not above passing some ribald comment when the mood should take her. 'I met him once when we first arrived in town. If my memory serves me correctly, he was forced to depart the capital very soon afterwards because of mounting debts.'

'There you have it in a nutshell, my lady! He's been playing deep of late, and Lord Alderman has flatly refused to honour his grandson's debts unless Toby proves that he is willing to mend his ways. Consequently, he's been blackmailed into remaining in the country, taking care of the estate, while the rest of the family are on a protracted visit to Scotland. I dare say, though, he'll take a bolt to town from time to time, just to relieve the tedium of country life, don't you know.'

'Before you betray any more of your friend's secrets, I think I should point out that young Mr Alderman's grandfather happens to be a close friend of my husband's,' the Countess warned, striving not to smile at the young lord's artless disclosures. 'As I'm sure you're aware, neither my daughter nor I am prone to gossiping, but we're only human, and do from time to time let fall snippets we have learned.'

'Oh, don't concern yourself, ma'am,' Nicholas responded with a dismissive wave of one shapely hand. 'Society has far more interesting things to gossip about at the moment. What with the continuing saga of Lady ''C'' and her poet friend, and all the speculation surrounding *The Wicked Marquis*, no one is likely to take much interest in Toby's comings and goings.'

'Yes, I've been hearing one or two things about

this book,' Sophia admitted, recalling something rather amusing that her friend Robina had disclosed the previous evening. 'It's commonly believed that certain characters have been drawn from real life.' It took a monumental effort, but she managed to refrain from divulging to her mother that 'dear' Hugo Perceval was believed to hold a prominent place between the book's covers, and that the author's vitriolic pen had been less than kind to him. 'I do not know how true it is, but I have also been told that the villain of the piece is based on none other than our oh, so charming neighbour.'

Her ladyship betrayed more than a faint interest on hearing this. 'Sywell…? Really…? Well, one cannot deny that he would admirably meet the requirements of the title.'

'He's certainly supposed to be the odds-on favourite,' Nicholas informed them. 'I cannot recall ever having met the chap myself. Something of a mad recluse, so I've been led to believe. Still,' he shrugged, 'I've always maintained that living in the country is grossly overrated, and that spending too much time watching the grass grow is bound to have an adverse effect on one in time. Why, you only have to look at m'sister to appreciate the truth of that. Gone peculiar in the attic since she turned her back on town life, and no mistake!

'Which reminds me of the reason for my visit today,' he continued, after his listeners had with some success managed to suppress their chuckles. 'My sis-

ter's home is less than ten miles from Toby
Alderman's place, so I decided I'd best pay a call,
otherwise I'd never hear the end of it if she ever discovered I'd been so close and hadn't taken the trouble
to pay her a visit. While I was there she reminded me
that it's our aunt Tabatha's birthday on Friday and
that I had foolishly promised to represent the family
by attending, as Constance herself will be unable to
do so this year owing to the fact that she'll be paying
a visit to Bath.'

'Well, the truth of the matter is I'd clean forgotten
about the wretched party, and that I'd foolishly offered to bring some friends along to stay the night
and help celebrate the event. I've been racking my
brains since returning to town trying to think of suitable people to ask.' He looked distinctly hopeful as
he gazed across at Sophia. 'And I was wondering
whether you would make up one of the small party
I'm taking from town?'

Although slightly surprised by Lord Risely's unexpected invitation, the Countess was not in the least
offended that she had not been included. Ordinarily,
of course, she would never have considered permitting her daughter to leave the capital in the middle of
the Season, and remain overnight in the house of a
woman who was to all intents and purposes a virtual
stranger, but given the strained atmosphere in the
house of late, she was not prepared to dismiss the idea
out of hand. After all, a little time away from the

Earl's all-seeing eye could do Sophia nothing but good, she decided, smiling warmly at their visitor.

'As you can imagine, the invitation has come as something of a surprise to us both, Lord Risely,' she announced while Sophia was silently rehearsing her polite refusal. 'As I'm sure you can appreciate, too, we shall need a little time to consider the matter. However, I think I should point out at the outset that I would never permit Sophia to travel to your aunt's home without a chaperon.'

'Certainly not,' his lordship agreed. 'I'm assured that my aunt intends to put her carriage at my disposal, and will ensure that all the young female guests are adequately chaperoned at all times.'

Lady Yardley could find no fault with these arrangements and, in turn, assured him that she would send a message to his lodgings informing him of her decision before the end of the day. Sophia was frankly astonished that her mother would even consider permitting her to go, and was not slow to voice her feelings once his lordship had taken his leave.

'But, Mama, you cannot have forgotten that it's the Meechams' ball on Friday. It is held to be one of the events of the Season, and not to be missed.'

'No, I hadn't forgotten, dear,' she responded, turning to her embroidery once more. 'And if you are set on going, then of course you must refuse the invitation.'

Rising to her feet, Sophia moved over to the window in time to see their unexpected visitor walking

out of the square. 'Strange,' she said, frowning
slightly, 'that the invitation didn't include you,
Mama.'

'No, I do not think so, dear,' she countered. 'Lady
Tabatha Risely has always had a reputation for being
slightly eccentric. She lives fairly comfortably, but if
my memory serves me correctly her house is not
large, so she's possibly restricted in the number of
people she can invite to stay at any one time.'

'Are you acquainted with her, Mama?'

'Slightly, yes, but I haven't seen her for a number
of years. She has turned seventy now, and rarely
comes to town.'

A dreadful possibility having taken possession of
her mind, Sophia was only vaguely aware of her
mother's response. 'You don't suppose Lord Nicholas
has developed a *tendre* for me, do you, Mama?' she
asked, sharing her fears, 'and a desire to introduce me
to his family is what really lies behind this unexpected invitation?'

'Would you be offended if I said most certainly
not?' Her ladyship cast her daughter a reassuring
smile. 'Rest easy, child. He likes you well enough,
but he's certainly not in love with you.'

Sophia almost sighed with relief as she rejoined her
mother on the sofa. 'In that case I shouldn't mind
getting away from the capital, if only for one night.
It has become quite warm, quite oppressive of late.
The country air will do me good.'

'Precisely what I thought myself,' the Countess

agreed. 'So I shall write informing Lord Nicholas that you accept, shall I?'

If Sophia's initial reaction to the unexpected invitation had been less than enthusiastic, by the time Friday had arrived, and she was standing at the parlour window awaiting the arrival of Lady Tabatha's carriage, she had begun to view the impending short sojourn away from town as nothing short of a godsend.

She was finding the changes in her father's personality increasingly difficult to accept and his continued presence in the evenings increasingly claustrophobic. Whenever she turned round, she would discover him hovering nearby, watching, scrutinising her every reaction to the different gentlemen who paid her varying degrees of attention. If he was hoping to see a sudden lovelorn expression take possession of her features, he would wait in vain, for although there were several personable young men in whose company she was more than content to while away an hour or so, no immaculately attired gentleman with whom she could happily spend the rest of her life had yet crossed her path.

And why this sudden urgency to see her married, anyway? she wondered, pondering anew on the question which had plagued her frequently during these past days. She recalled clearly enough that, when they had first arrived in town, the Earl's main concern had seemed to be a determination to protect her from fortune-hunters. Perhaps, in part, this was still the case, but she couldn't help feeling that at some point during the recent past the Earl had, for reasons known only to himself, developed an almost obsessive desire to see her married, or at the very least betrothed, before the Season was over.

She shook her head, still quite unable to account for this drastic change in him. But life was not all doom and gloom, she reminded herself, flatly refusing to allow her father's continuing unreasonable behaviour to mar totally the pleasure she was surprisingly still managing to attain from this, her first Season in the capital. After all, she could still rely on her mother's unfailing support. Thank goodness! How lucky she was too to have friends like Robina Perceval about her to confide in…And then, of course, she now had Ben…

How she had missed him during this past week! she was forced silently to concede. At least, though, they had managed to exchange a few words whenever she had returned to the stables after her daily ride. That wonderful, spontaneous, wide smile of his, always preceding a few reassuring words, never failed to raise her flagging spirits.

Ben continued to be firmly convinced that her father's present melancholy state would not last indefinitely. And one never knew, perhaps he was right, she decided, absently watching a very smart curricle and pair turn into the square. Ben's judgement had most certainly not been at fault when he had predicted that the gossips would swiftly forget about a young lady's seeming infatuation with her groom once they had been provided with tastier morsels to drool over. Lady Caroline Lamb's scandalous exploits, together with those of another high-ranking female personage whose name was being linked these days with a certain member of the royal household, had definitely kept the tattle-mongers' tongues busy of late. Not once during the past two or three days could Sophia recall observing any sly glances cast in her direction. So perhaps it was safe now to resume her daily rides with Ben once she had returned to town, she thought, watching the curricle which had driven into the square a few moments before pull up outside the house.

Sophia had little difficulty in recognising the tall figure jumping down from the smart equipage, once a servant had rushed from the house to hold the horses' heads, and felt her spirits begin to flag a little when Lord Nicholas, not looking too happy himself, entered the room a few moments later. 'Has the party been cancelled?' she asked, deciding that this must be the reason for his visit.

'No, no! Nothing like that,' he hurriedly assured her, casting a furtive glance over his shoulder at Cardew, who remained standing sentinel-like by the door, determined it seemed to protect his young mistress from the unwholesome attentions of young men. 'Thing is my aunt's carriage hasn't turned up. Should have arrived over an hour ago. Can only imagine it must have met with an accident.'

Sophia considered the matter for a moment before proposing that she make the journey in her father's own well-sprung travelling-carriage, but she could discern by his expression that his lordship was not precisely in favour of this, even before he said, 'No need for that. Old Freddy Fortescue and his sister are taking a bolt to the country today. Their grandmother lives only a stone's throw away from my aunt's place, so we can beg a lift with them.' He took a moment to glance at the clock. 'Chances are they won't have left town yet. With any luck we'll catch them before they set off if we hurry.'

He turned, about to retrace his steps into the hall, only to discover his way blocked by the solid figure of the butler. 'I think it behoves me to remind you, my lady,' Cardew remarked at his most haughty, 'that her ladyship gave strict instructions before she left the house earlier that I was to hand you personally into Lady Tabatha Risely's carriage, and no other.'

'Yes, but as you've already heard, Cardew, for some reason Lady Tabatha's carriage hasn't arrived, so stop creating unnecessary difficulties by delaying me further and have my overnight bag taken out to his lordship's curricle at once.'

'You know, this man of yours has a point, there. Must think of the proprieties,' Nicholas put in, earning himself a faint look of approval from the punctilious retainer. 'It's all very well for you to travel with me as far as the Fortescues' place, no harm in that at all. But supposing Freddy and his sister have already left? Can't go careering after them with you sitting beside me, unchaperoned, now can I?'

He appeared to ponder over the problem for a moment. 'I tell you what, we'll take that groom of yours along with us. Then, if someone does observe us leaving the capital, it'll not cause a stir.'

Having anticipated a relatively peaceful afternoon, Ben was mildly surprised when he received the summons to present himself at the front entrance without delay. He knew for a fact that the Earl and Countess were at that very moment being conveyed about the town by the dutiful Trapp in the light town carriage. Sophia, he had been reliably informed, was spending the afternoon and evening out of the capital, so he was hardly expecting to see her, as he rounded the corner from the mews, being assisted into a curricle by an instantly recognisable figure in an expertly tailored bottle-green coat.

Benedict's suspicions were instantly aroused. His brother, as far as he could recall, had never betrayed the least inclination to join the sporting-mad Corinthian set. Feather-edging a corner with less than an inch to spare simply wasn't Nicholas's style at all. So what, he asked himself, was his young brother doing in charge of such a bang-up-to-date turnout which was almost certainly not his own? More importantly, what was the young reprobate doing with the future Duchess of Sharnbrook, when the darling girl ought to have been away from the city long since, enjoying the sweet country air? he wondered, his suspicions increasing alarmingly when he noticed that Nicholas seemed very reluctant to meet his eye.

Sophia experienced no such reservations, and smiled brightly down at him. 'You are here to lend me countenance, Ben,' she told him when he at last stood beside the carriage and had cast her an enquiring glance. 'Lord Nicholas and Cardew, here,' she added, as the butler placed her overnight bag beneath the seat himself, 'seem to think that my reputation will suffer if I am seen leaving town in an open carriage. Silly, don't you think?'

'No, I do not,' Benedict responded with the brutal honesty to which Sophia had grown quite accustomed. 'And might I point out that I am a groom and not a duenna. Furthermore, my lady, you should not be contemplating leaving town in this equipage at all!'

In any other circumstances Cardew might have taken the groom roundly to task for daring to answer his young mistress in such a disrespectful fashion. The fact of the matter was, however, he wholeheartedly agreed, and couldn't bring himself to play the hypocrite by administering a strong reprimand.

Nicholas, on the other hand, experienced no such qualms, and gained a deal of perverse pleasure in ordering his big brother to mind his tongue before commanding him in the same brusque manner to climb up on the back of the curricle. He gave him only sufficient time to do so before picking up the reins and giving the splendid pair of matched greys the office to start.

They swept out of the square, a silent trio, each absorbed in his or her own thoughts, but it was not very long before Benedict's curiosity got the better of him and, swallowing his ire, forced himself to enquire where they were bound.

'Curzon Street,' Nicholas answered, secretly smiling at the clipped tones. Unless he very much mistook the matter, big brother would dearly love to strangle him. 'And with any luck we'll get there in time.'

'In time for what, dare I ask?'

'It appears to me, my good man,' Nicholas responded, mimicking quite beautifully the haughty disapproval shown by the Yardleys' very correct butler a short while earlier, 'that you have the gall to dare anything. I shall take leave to inform you that you are an impertinent devil!' He caught what sounded suspiciously like a suppressed feminine chuckle. 'I wonder that you bear with such insolence, Lady Sophia,' he continued, enjoying himself hugely, though at the same time well aware he would probably pay dearly later if his brother managed to get him alone. 'I certainly would not. The rogue would not last five minutes in my household. Or any other, come to that!'

'Ben is not in the common way, certainly,' Sophia was forced to concede, glancing over her shoulder in time to see her groom casting the gentleman on the seat beside her a dagger-look. 'We are hoping to catch some friends of Lord Nicholas before they leave town, Ben. Then I shall be suitably chaperoned, and you can return to Berkeley Square.'

'And if you are not in time, my lady?'

Ben's question was not an unreasonable one, but Sophia found herself quite unable to answer it, and turned to his lordship for guidance. 'Oh, there'll be no problem,' Nicholas announced, sounding sublimely unconcerned. 'Even if they have already left the house, I dare swear we'll catch up with them long before they've reached the outskirts of the capital.'

Unfortunately this did not turn out to be the case. Which certainly did not surprise Benedict in the least, for the perfectly matched greys were not once encouraged to go above a very moderate pace.

Of course his brother might have an excellent reason for maintaining such a slow speed, Benedict decided, as they left the last of the straggling dwellings on the outskirts of the capital behind. The turn-out, he strongly suspected, belonged to one of his brother's friends, and Nicholas was no doubt taking extra care to ensure that neither carriage nor horses sustained any damage at his hands. Or maybe he was hoping to cover as many miles as possible with the same team, and was therefore not overtaxing the greys. Both explanations were plausible, and yet he could not rid himself of the ever-growing conviction that his brother was bent on some mischief.

He turned his attention to the other occupant of the seat, and realised suddenly that during the last few miles Sophia had grown increasingly quiet, and was now looking rather thoughtful. His brother might, indeed, be indulging in some wicked prank, but Benedict doubted very much that his future bride was a party to it. No, unless he much mistook the matter, she was as puzzled as he was himself as to why Nicholas had made no attempt whatsoever to catch up with his friends the Fortescues.

They continued at the same monotonous snail's pace for a further twenty minutes or so, during which time they were overtaken by a variety of carriages including a lumbering coach. Then Nicholas, quite without warning, announced his intention of putting up for a change and, betraying an element of skill, turned the curricle with a flourish into the yard of a very busy posting house.

'Might I be permitted to know where we are bound, my lady?' Benedict asked while his brother, who had swiftly alighted, was busily engaged in issuing orders to an ostler.

'To the home of Lady Tabatha Risely, a relative of his lordship's,' she enlightened him, not finding his curiosity remotely suspicious. 'If we ever manage to get there, that is.'

Not even by the raising of one of his expressive brows did Benedict betray the least surprise at their intended destination, though he found it impossible not to chuckle at his beloved's hint of sarcasm.

Sophia found the deep masculine rumble immensely reassuring and turned in the seat to look directly at the man whom she had never been able to view in the light of a servant. 'I'm so very glad you're here, Ben,' she told him, unashamedly betraying her thoughts. 'I should feel distinctly uneasy if you were not.'

Out of the corner of her eye she noticed Nicholas slinking away to disappear into the inn. 'Does it seem to you that his lordship has made no attempt whatsoever to overtake his friend's carriage? The Fortescues' servants assured us that the carriage left not half an hour before we arrived at the house. We ought to have caught up with them long since. Most certainly would have done so if you'd held the ribbons!' She was struck by a sudden thought. 'I've a mind to suggest that you do take over. And where in heaven's name has Lord Nicholas got to now!' she snapped, allowing mounting irritation to surface.

Something in her expression must have betrayed her feelings of pique, for Nicholas apologised for keeping her waiting the instant he returned. 'Just popped inside to ascertain whether or not my friend Freddy has already passed this way.'

'It must have been so long ago that I'm surprised the landlord could remember,' she retorted, and it took a monumental effort but Nicholas did somehow manage to preserve his countenance.

'The Fortescues do keep fine cattle, so perhaps I was slightly foolish to attempt to overtake them,' he acknowledged in a voice which shook only very slightly. 'I shan't, however, continue the attempt. Nor shall I delay further in the hope of seeing Aunt Tabatha's carriage come bowling towards us. Instead, I'll try to make up for lost time by taking a little short cut I know,' and so saying he turned off the post road.

They continued for several miles down a series of narrow, twisting lanes. As far as Sophia was concerned, the county of Surrey might have been a foreign land. She had no idea of where they were, nor did she even know in which direction they were heading, now that the sun had disappeared behind a thick blanket of cloud. Benedict, too, was not familiar with this route, for although he had paid numerous visits to the home of his elderly maiden aunt in the distant past, he had invariably travelled along the main post roads whenever making the journey.

'I don't think it would be a bad idea at all if we took the time to stop for a short while in order to refresh ourselves,' Nicholas suggested as they reached a sleepy little village where a rambling thatched inn, nestling among some trees, stood opposite the church. 'I've been here before, and can assure you the fare is excellent. I might even be persuaded to treat that impertinent groom of yours to a tankard,' he could not resist adding before bringing his horses to a halt and, ignoring his brother's loud, derisive snort, escorted Sophia into the spotlessly clean, low-ceilinged building.

When his brother, having seen to the comfort of the horses, sauntered in a few minutes later, Nicholas decided that he might as well have been invisible for all the notice that was taken of him. Over the rim of his tankard he studied his companions, and for the second time in the space of a few hours found himself having to exert a monumental effort to maintain his countenance. How his brother had managed to remain employed for this length of time eluded him completely. Benedict was not remotely deferential. In fact, for a 'servant' he was appallingly rude! Yet it was quite evident that Sophia didn't appear to mind, or didn't appear to notice, one or the other.

He shook his head. They certainly made an unconventional couple—the Earl's daughter and her golden-haired groom. At least he didn't doubt that they would make a perfect couple, providing nothing went wrong with his well-laid plans!

Chapter Eleven

When it happened he really ought to have been prepared, ought to have been expecting something to occur sooner or later, and yet Benedict would have been the first to admit that at the time he was taken completely by surprise. One moment they were bowling along the narrow, twisting country lane, hoping against hope that they could manage to reach their destination before that threatening dark bank of clouds, which had been slowly gathering from the west, released its moisture; the next moment they were in the ditch, viewing the landscape from a very peculiar angle, all helplessly watching the offside wheel rolling away along the road ahead of them.

Fortunately none of them was hurt. One of the bays, however, had not been so lucky, and had sustained a slightly strained hock. Although the injury was not serious, the animal could no longer be expected to pull the carriage, even if the equipage were roadworthy. Which it most definitely was not!

At the time Benedict considered that his young brother had had no choice but to take such swift and drastic action in order to avoid a collision with the oncoming carriage, which had been travelling far too swiftly for safety along such narrow lanes. It was only a short time later, after Nicholas had suggested that he journey back to the inn with the horses, and Benedict and Sophia seek shelter until his return at the cottage which stood a little further along the road, that Benedict's suspicions were first aroused, and he began seriously to consider the possibility that the unfortunate occurrence might not have been the innocent accident which it had first appeared.

He glanced over his shoulder in time to see Nicholas, mounted on the healthy bay, and carefully leading the injured animal, disappear round the bend in the road, and decided that it was a stroke of great good fortune that they had met the other carriage along that particular stretch of road, for it was the only place, for some considerable distance, wide enough for two vehicles to pass with care. Chance, or pure contrivance? he couldn't help asking himself. Was it a happy coincidence also that there just happened to be a cottage nearby where shelter might be sought? His eyes narrowed. It was all beginning to appear rather smoky, he decided, blithely entering the cottage after receiving no response to his second knock.

Sophia, having little experience of the conditions endured by the unfortunate poor, cast an interested glance round the one-roomed dwelling and was favourably impressed. 'Well, I must say, this is all very clean and cosy.'

Yes, a little too clean and cosy, Benedict decided, his suspicions increasing with every passing second. Not even at Sharnbrook did the estate workers live in such comfort. White linen sheets, feather pillows and what felt suspiciously like a horsehair mattress were not the usual trappings of cottage-dwellers. And how many working men, he wondered, unable to suppress a wry grin as he turned his attention to the foodstuffs placed on the wooden table, could afford the luxury of a fine claret to wash down their bread and cheese? Really, Nicholas was stretching things a little too far for authenticity!

He shook his head. Undoubtedly these items had been carried here from some large house nearby, solely for his and Sophia's comfort. Furthermore, he considered it pretty safe to assume that whoever it was who had so thoughtfully catered for their needs had not contemplated that their stay would be of short duration.

'We may as well make ourselves comfortable while we await his lordship's return,' Benedict suggested, adding a log to the sizeable fire some considerate soul had prepared in readiness for their arrival. He didn't add that he would be amazed if they saw any sign of Nicholas before morning, or anybody else, come to that. No, unless he was very much mistaken, he was supposed to take advantage of a night spent alone here with Sophia. Strangely enough he had never once considered the possibility of seduction as a means by which he might attain his ends. He watched her seat herself in the rocking chair by the hearth. But he was only human, and she was a very lovely young woman...

'Are you contemplating a drastic drop in temperature, Ben?' Sophia enquired as he absently added a further sizeable log to the blaze. She edged the rocking chair a little further away from the hearth. 'Though perhaps you're wise,' she added as the first spots of rain began to trickle their way down the small window. 'Lord Nicholas is likely to arrive at the inn soaked to the skin, poor man.'

Poor Nicholas? Benedict silently echoed, unable to suppress a further wry grin. Would she be quite so concerned over the young lord's well-being if she began to suspect the truth? There was not a doubt in his own mind now that Nicholas, no doubt aided and abetted by some close friend living not so very far from here, had planned this escapade down to the finest detail.

Suddenly experiencing his first pangs of conscience, Benedict did not find it at all easy to meet that trustful green-eyed gaze. 'There's no guarantee,' he warned in an attempt to prepare her, 'that his lordship will be able to hire another carriage. In fact, it is most unlikely that he shall. That place we stopped at is just a village inn, remember, not a posting-house. He's unlikely to attain much joy there.'

'True, but might not the innkeeper own a gig?' she suggested, after giving the matter a moment's thought.

'It's possible, certainly. But whether or not he'd be willing to hire it out to a perfect stranger is quite another matter.'

Sophia regarded him in mild surprise. 'I do not believe that his lordship is a stranger to that particular innkeeper or his wife. Didn't you notice the friendly terms on which they appeared to be?'

He had, but he could have wished that she had been less observant, for it was quite obvious that she was expecting Nicholas to attain all the help he needed with little difficulty. Which was possibly no less than the truth, though Benedict strongly suspected that his young brother had already attained all the aid he required with the deliberate sabotaging of the curricle, and would require no further assistance until morning.

Fixing his eyes on an imaginary spot on the floor, he began to ponder over how best to voice his suspicions, and swiftly discovered that he could not bring himself to be the one to crush those childlike beliefs she still managed to retain. He didn't wish to be the one to tell her that people whom she liked and admired could and perhaps often did behave in a less than honourable way on occasions; that people were not simply good or evil, but a complex mixture of both. She had, he knew, suspected all along that Nicholas had deliberately tooled the curricle at a very slow pace, but it would never cross her mind to suppose for a moment that the accident which had resulted in their being alone together here had been anything other than an unfortunate mishap; it would never cross her mind to suppose for a moment that everything that had happened to her since she left Berkeley Square had been carefully planned down to the finest detail and that the honourable young lord whom she liked so much had never had the least intention of taking her to his Aunt Tabatha's home.

'I'm not in the least familiar with this part of the country, are you, Ben?'

Drawing his eyes away from the imaginary spot on the floor, and his mind back to the present, Benedict searched in vain for a hint of concern in that lovely face of hers. She appeared, as she slowly began to untie the ribbons of her fashionable bonnet, completely undisturbed by her present unfortunate predicament, accepting her lot with a quaint and dignified resignation.

'I haven't any real idea of exactly where we are, no,' he admitted. 'This place is undoubtedly an estate-worker's cottage, so there's bound to be a big house somewhere nearby. When the rain eases off a little, I'll see if I can locate its whereabouts, and get help.'

Once again she made no attempt to hide her surprise. 'Do you think that's wise? Supposing his lordship returns while we're away. Yes, I did say we,' she added, smiling at the sudden raising of those expressive masculine brows, a trait which she had come to consider most endearing. 'You don't suppose that

I'd calmly stay here on my own, and permit you to go wandering off to heaven knows where? Besides, the tenant might well return while you're away. There's no saying what sort of person I'd find myself having to deal with.' She glanced about her, as something at last occurred to her as odd. 'Though I must say, whoever lives here does keep the place very clean and tidy. Are all cottages kept this well, Ben? I must confess to being quite ignorant about such things.'

'In my experience, no,' he answered, smiling in spite of the fact that he was rapidly becoming annoyed by the situation in which he now found himself through no fault of his own.

He moved over to the window, and was appalled to discover that the rain, far from abating, was increasing. Confound his brother for an interfering young cub! he cursed silently. If Nicholas had been standing beside him, he would quite cheerfully have throttled him. He didn't doubt for a moment that Nicholas's actions had been prompted by nothing more than deep brotherly concern. But hadn't the headstrong young fool even taken the time to consider the very real possibility that Sophia just might not care for his big brother enough to want to marry him? Worse still, that she might consider a ruined reputation favourable to being tied for life to someone she could never respect?

It was a heart-rending possibility, but one that was much better faced, if not by Nicholas, then certainly

by himself. Just as it was better to face the fact that
some deep and wholly dishonourable part of him was
not sorry to have been granted this golden opportunity
to attain what his heart most desired. Nor could he
deny the fact that he was not totally unwilling to listen
to that demon of temptation urging him to take advantage of this situation, goading him to seduce her
now and to the devil with the consequences! He had
managed to resist thus far the prompting of his baser
instincts…But for how much longer could he continue to do so?

By the time Ben had lit the tallow candles on the
mantelshelf, and they had eaten their fill of the simple
yet wholesome fare, Sophia was well and truly re-
signed to spending her very first night in a humble
cottage, and a part of her was determined to enjoy
the novel experience, too. Although the rain had begun to abate some little time ago, it was far too dark
now to contemplate an expedition outside in order to
discover some larger dwelling where they might attain aid in reaching their destination, and she had sen-
sibly abandoned all hope of seeing his lordship again
until morning.

Drawing her eyes away from the flames dancing in
the hearth, she looked across at Ben, seated opposite
on the wooden settle. It might have been pure imagination, but she sensed a suppressed tension about
him now that had not been apparent when they had
first arrived at the cottage. Concern over her reputa-

tion might well be the cause, she decided, unable to suppress a smile. How strange that she was not in the least perturbed; had not once experienced the least trepidation throughout the entire eventful afternoon and evening, simply because that particular man had been with her.

She didn't even attempt to analyse this rather startling truth; instead, she merely echoed her initial thoughts by remarking quite casually, 'I think we must face the fact, Ben, that his lordship might be unable to rescue us until morning.'

He paused in the act of adding a further log to the blaze, his blue eyes penetrating, and glinting with some emotion that was difficult to interpret, as he turned them momentarily in her direction. 'You do not appear unduly disturbed. Doesn't it trouble you being alone here with me, Sophia?'

What made her start, caught her completely off guard, was not the bluntness of the question—she had grown accustomed to this directness quite early in their association—but the fact that he had deliberately made free with her given name, and that it had sounded so natural coming from his lips.

'No, of course it does not,' she assured him, forcing the words through a mouth that for some inexplicable reason had suddenly grown uncomfortably dry.

Rising from the chair, she went across the small room and swiftly eased the slight discomfort by helping herself from what remained of the bottle of wine resting on the table. She knew she really ought to reprimand him for such familiarity, but instead found herself asking, 'Why do you suppose that I might be troubled?'

An unmistakable challenging gleam sprang into blue eyes. 'Because I'm a man…a groom, perhaps, but no less a man than—shall we say—a marquis or a duke. And because we'll be spending the whole night together…and quite alone.' In one lithe movement he had risen from the settle and was slowly coming towards her. 'It might be wise for you to take a moment or two to consider the consequences.'

'Consequences?' she echoed, wondering why her heart had suddenly decided to attempt to beat its way through her ribcage when she remained quite unafraid, and steadfastly refused to move even though he had come to stand so close behind her that she could feel his warm breath fanning the tiny curls feathering the nape of her neck.

'If you imagine my father is likely to come after you brandishing a pistol and demanding you do the honourable thing, you may rest easy,' she assured him, astonished herself at the unmistakable note of disappointment which had found its way quite without design into her voice. 'Had you been a marquis now…well, that would be a different matter entirely.'

'To your father, perhaps, but not to you.' His fingers were on her upper arms, turning her round gently yet firmly to face him squarely. 'It is the man you would care about, not his wealth or his social position.' The glinting devilment in his eyes had disappeared completely, leaving a gaze so intense that she found it impossible to draw her own away. 'But supposing your father, for whatever reason, did insist on a match between us, Sophia, would you try to dissuade him?'

No, never! her heart responded with such vehemence that her mind refused even to attempt to deny the truth of it. It was madness, perhaps, but she could think of no one with whom she would rather spend the rest of her days than this tall enigmatic stranger who had unexpectedly come into her life, and who by degrees so subtle that she had hardly been aware of it had become totally indispensable to her happiness. Quite simply she loved him, and had for some little time.

The realisation, sudden though it was, in no way surprised her. Her lips parted, but the assurances that her heart longed to make were smothered by the firm mouth which suddenly covered her own.

No thought of resistance crossed her mind, then or moments later, when she found herself being pressed inexorably back against the softness of the horsehair mattress, one powerful, muscular leg moving across her thighs keeping her a very willing prisoner, while masculine lips and fingers were working a particular kind of intoxicating magic on her highly responsive body. The chaste salutes she had permitted a few honoured members of the opposite sex to place upon her fingers and proffered cheek in the past had in no way prepared her for this peerless display of masculine passion. And her reaction to it was no less shocking. Instead of striving to attempt at least a token display of maidenly modesty, she was actively encouraging him to take further liberties by easing her body into a position whereby he was better able to reach the tiny buttons at the neckline of her dress and ease the restricting garment down over her shoulders.

She found herself quite unable to control the shivers of pleasure rippling through her as Ben's right hand began to explore the fine bones of her shoulder, and then moved lower to trace the rounded contour of her breast. She would never have believed it possible that the feather-light touch of masculine fingers could create such a wealth of wholly pleasurable physical sensations, blocking the mind, suppressing all rational thoughts save one.

'I love you,' she murmured, so softly that she was hardly aware that she had spoken, but instantly aware of the change in him. She felt him stiffen, felt those magical fingers still, before he raised his head to stare down into her face, his eyes glinting with a strange mixture of triumph and hard determination. Then he was on his feet and, easily avoiding the tentative hand she stretched out towards him, was moving out of reach, muttering words which made little sense at the time, but which she was to remember very well in the weeks, months, and years to come.

'No, not this way,' he said again, as though desperately striving to convince himself. 'Perhaps I'm mad. No doubt my enterprising young brother will think me mad…but, no matter. I cannot allow it to happen…not this way.'

Sophia regarded him in silence as he reached out to grasp the mantelshelf with those fingers that had wrought such havoc on her senses only moments before. 'Ben, I don't understand you.' She felt like a child, hurt and confused, being punished for doing something, though it knew not what. 'Have I done something wrong?'

He did not attempt to answer, and she couldn't help wondering whether her immodest lack of restraint might not be at the root of this sudden change in him. Instinctively she reached for the neckline of her dress, and tried to set the garment to rights as unobtrusively and swiftly as possible, which was certainly no easy task as all her fingers seemed to have been replaced by thumbs.

'I do love you, Ben,' she assured him when she felt more able to face him again. 'I would never have allowed you…I mean, I would not have permitted you…'

'I know what you mean.' He did take the trouble to look at her then, and although she could not be perfectly certain of precisely what he was thinking, or feeling, she could detect no hint of disgust or revulsion in his eyes. 'That is precisely why I'm not prepared to let it happen this way. I must approach your father in the accepted manner. I want him…and you to be given the choice.'

'What!' Sophia gaped across at him, unable to believe that such an intelligent man had uttered anything so foolish. 'Ben, you must be all about in your head…Or I am!' Which was highly likely, as her poor temples had begun to throb. 'Papa will never give his consent. Never, do you hear!'

'No?' He appeared not in the least convinced, nor, it had to be said, very concerned, either. In fact, if anything, he looked merely highly amused. 'Well, I hope you're wrong, but if not, we must just trust that sense will prevail and that he'll come round given time.'

'He won't!' A simpleton could not have mistaken the conviction in her voice. 'You don't know my father. Where do you suppose I inherited my stubborn, determined streak? I've told you before what it's been like at home during these past two or three weeks,' she reminded him, wondering why those broad shoulders appeared to be shaking with suppressed laughter. 'It's been a constant battle of wills. I have through various stratagems remained the victor thus far, but there's no saying that that state of affairs will continue for very much longer. For some reason Papa seems determined to see me suitably settled before the Season comes to an end, and he isn't a man to accept defeat easily.'

'That being the case, he ought to be delighted when I approach him with my offer.'

Her ludicrously crestfallen expression was almost his undoing. He knew precisely what was passing through that pretty little head of hers, and wanted nothing more than to assure her that everything would be all right when he did eventually approach the Earl to ask for her hand, but he remained firm. The lovely Sophia, spoilt and indulged from birth, needed to be taught that she could not have everything she wanted in life, that she must be prepared to make concessions, and, most important of all, she had to be persuaded to abandon those few remaining girlish fancies which she was trying to take with her into womanhood and accept the reality of who she was and what she was.

'Of course I do realise there is always the possibility that he may take me in dislike, may not approve of me, in which case when we do marry we must be prepared to forfeit your dowry.'

For the first time there was a faint hint of uncertainty in her eyes, and in her voice, too, as she asked, 'Would that matter to you so very much? It certainly would not to me.'

'It wouldn't, eh?'

'No, it wouldn't. I would willingly forfeit my inheritance in order to marry the man I love.'

'Very affecting!' He didn't spare her feelings, couldn't spare her feelings if he wanted to be certain of winning her, and raised his eyes ceilingwards. 'So, you suppose that love is the only thing that's important, eh?'

'Ben, what's wrong?' Her evident anxiety was almost more than he could bear. 'Don't you wish to marry me?'

'More than you realise, my darling, but we'll leave

that for the moment. Let us discuss instead just how good a wife you'd make for a hard-working groom.'

Planting his feet firmly apart, he folded his arms across his chest, and looked her over, just as though she were some prize filly up for sale at Tattersall's. 'You're pleasing on the eye, and there's no mistaking that air of breeding. But a sensible man wouldn't purchase a thoroughbred to pull a plough.'

He could easily detect the first stirring of her temper, even before she advised him in no uncertain terms to keep a civil tongue in his head.

'I doubt you can cook,' he continued, just as though she had not spoken, 'and I doubt you've ever held so much as a broom in your hand, either. I would be astonished if you've ever attempted to starch a cravat, or wash an item of clothing, come to that. All in all you'd be of precious little use to a poor man, my darling, and I think any would do well to consider very carefully before contemplating taking you to wife.'

To Sophia the implication seemed perfectly plain: the man whom she had just discovered that she loved, the man for whom she would quite happily have sacrificed everything in order to be with, was himself having second thoughts about her!

She felt bitterly hurt, especially after the loving exchange which had taken place between them only a short time before, and thoroughly humiliated by the catalogue of what he evidently perceived as her shortcomings. She had never considered herself to be a vindictive person, but she found she was totally unable to suppress the overwhelming need to hurt and humiliate him in return.

Tapping into that deep well of feminine pride, she rose from the bed and faced him squarely. 'I think, all things considered, we would both do well to think long and hard before making a decision which in the future we might come to regret,' she announced, sounding every inch the haughty aristocrat. 'You most especially, because it must be perfectly plain that you cannot possibly continue as my groom, not after what has taken place between us.'

'I could not agree more,' he obligingly concurred. 'Furthermore, I have no intention of spending the night with you in this cottage, but shall relieve you of one of your blankets and await the arrival of dawn on the porch.' And so saying, he did no more than whisk one of the covers off the bed and move over to the door, remaining only to murmur what sounded suspiciously like, 'Goodnight, Duchess.'

Several times before she eventually fell asleep Sophia was on the point of calling out to him to come back inside and spend the night on the settle before the fire, but stubborn pride prevented her. Long before she awoke to find bright sunlight filtering through the cottage window, she had come to regret hasty words spoken in anger, and was determined to persuade him to stay, certain that they could find some way out of their difficulties. But it was already too late. Although she wasn't to know it as she threw off the covers and hurriedly scrambled into her crumpled gown, Benjamin Rudgely was already heading off down the road on a borrowed mount and out of her life for ever.

Chapter Twelve

'Flagrant ingratitude!' One or two of the breakfast dishes came perilously close to ending on the floor as the Earl of Yardley gave vent to his annoyance by bringing the flat of his hand down rather hard on the table. 'What else can you call it, pray? I knew at the time I was being less than sensible to consider taking the fellow on without so much as a reference, but, kind-hearted fool that I am, I did so against my better judgement. And how does the rogue repay my generosity?' he demanded of neither of his listeners in particular. 'I'll tell you how—by taking himself off without so much as a by your leave, and leaving us short-handed! Ungrateful scoundrel!'

The Countess, having listened with a sympathetic ear to her husband's justifiable grievances against the errant groom, Benjamin Rudgely, could not forbear a smile. It was a pleasure to have her husband's company at breakfast again, even if he did on this particular occasion happen to be bemoaning life's iniquities. At least, she reminded herself, these instances of ill-humour were becoming far less frequent of late, and although she could hardly say that he was any-where near back to his normally even-tempered self quite yet, there had been a noticeable improvement in his attitude during the past few days.

'His actions might have been, shall we say, a trifle thoughtless, dear, but I think it's unjust to brand him a scoundrel,' she pointed out, fair-minded as always. 'It was inconsiderate of Master Rudgely, I'll own, not to take the trouble to work his notice, but at least he did not help himself to the family's silver, or anyone else's as far as we're aware, before he disappeared.'

'True enough,' his lordship conceded, his frown of disapproval marginally fading. 'But it's still deuced odd.' His eyes moved from his wife to the third oc-cupant of the table. 'And you can shed no more light on the matter, Sophia?'

'She's already told us all she can, dear,' her lady-ship put in, instantly coming to her daughter's aid. 'If anyone should bemoan the disappearance of Benjamin Rudgely, then it is our daughter.' She cast a sympathetic smile across the table. 'You had grown fond of him, hadn't you dear?'

'Very,' Sophia responded, marvelling at her con-tinuing self-control and—yes—feeling more than just a little proud of herself too.

Not once since she had woken that morning to dis-cover not Ben sitting on the veranda outside the cot-tage, but Lord Nicholas Risely and the wife of the innkeeper whose hostelry they had patronised briefly the previous afternoon, had she betrayed to anyone the searing heartache which never left her for a moment. She recalled clearly that Ben had always considered ladies of her class who indulged in forceful displays of emotion in public faintly vulgar. She had always listened with interest to his opinions and, quite surprisingly, had very nearly always agreed with his point of view.

She was fast coming to accept too, painfully hard though it was, that everything he had said during the unforgettable night spent in that cottage just one short week ago, one week which seemed more like a year, had been no less than the truth. Only in fairy tales did princesses marry frogs. Only foolish childish fantasies could permit ladies of quality to marry their grooms and live happily ever after. Oh, yes, he had been painfully all too right, she reminded herself silently. She could only hope that one day she might be granted the opportunity to tell him so—tell him that although she loved him still, and perhaps always would, a match between them could never have taken place.

'I do not believe there is anything I can add to what I've already told you,' Sophia confirmed, abruptly abandoning her reverie when she became aware of two pairs of eyes firmly turned in her direction. 'I've already explained the reason why I decided to take Ben with me. Although,' she amended 'to be perfectly honest with you, I do believe it was Lord Nicholas's suggestion. When his aunt's carriage failed to turn up, he felt I couldn't possibly accompany him about town without even a groom to lend me countenance.'

His lordship tutted. 'Lady Tabatha Risely always

was an idiotish female. Fancy forgetting to send the carriage for one of her guests when she'd promised faithfully to do so!'

'Perhaps there is some excuse,' his wife pointed out. 'After all, she has turned seventy, dear.'

His lordship's grey brows rose sharply. 'Well? And what of it? So have I turned seventy, and there's nothing wrong with my memory.'

'No, dear,' the Countess thankfully agreed. 'But you are rather exceptional. And as you've already remarked, Lady Tabatha has always had a tendency to be—er—slightly scatty. Thank heavens it doesn't run in the family! Lord Nicholas, the dear boy, showed great presence of mind insisting on taking our groom along, although I could have wished he had not taken it into his head to travel the whole distance to his aunt's house in an open carriage when he failed to catch up with his friends.'

'No, perhaps that wasn't the wisest course of action,' Sophia was forced to concede, 'but as I've already explained, Mama, by the time we'd stopped at that inn to change horses, it would have taken us just as much time to return here to collect the travelling-carriage as it would to travel on to Lady Tabatha's home.'

Sophia had considered the explanation a reasonable one, and both her parents seemed to have accepted it as such. 'I didn't realise that his lordship hadn't intended staying the night at his aunt's home, but had arranged to stay with his friend Toby Alderman who resides nearby,' she went on to explain, remembering clearly what Lord Nicholas had advised her to say in the event her parents should ever enquire further.

Somehow her numbed brain had managed to assimilate everything he had said to her during the short journey back to town in Toby Alderman's carriage, with the landlady of that small inn acting as chaperon. Their return to town could not have appeared more proper, and he had had every intention of its remaining so by the wonderful tale he had concocted.

Sophia had accepted his suggestion at the time without question, Ben's unexpected disappearance having left her so numbed that she had been in no fit state to do otherwise. It was only during the past day or so that she had begun to wonder why Lord Nicholas had been so set against her offering the true account of what had taken place. After all, nothing very improper had occurred. Ben had spent the entire night out on the veranda. Nevertheless she had given her word to Nicholas, and she had no intention of breaking it now.

'When his lordship suggested that he take Ben along with him to spend the night at the Aldermans' place, I never thought anything of it. As you remarked yourself, Mama, Lady Tabatha's house isn't large, and she really didn't want to be troubled with the added burden of having to cater for unnecessary servants. Of course it came as a shock when I discovered Ben had taken himself off without telling a soul where he was bound.'

'Yes, I'm sure it must have, dear. Most odd of him!' Her ladyship, looking decidedly thoughtful, took a moment to finish the contents of her cup before enquiring, 'I do not suppose Lord Nicholas has managed to discover anything further?'

'Not as far as I am aware, Mama. He knows that part of the country very well, and has promised to make enquiries. As you know, the whole town is now talking of his brother's return, and I believe Lord Nicholas has gone into Hampshire to spend a few days with the Duke at Sharnbrook. I'll see him when he returns to town, and find out if he's discovered anything further then.'

'It's a great pity young Rudgely did take it into his head to leave us,' his lordship unexpectedly remarked. 'I wish now I'd taken the trouble to get to know him a little. Apart from passing the time of day on one or two occasions, I don't believe we exchanged more than half a dozen words during the whole time he was here. Trapp came to see me the other morning,' he went on to divulge. 'Very concerned he was that the lad hadn't even bothered to return to collect his few belongings.'

Dry-eyed and remaining remarkably composed, Sophia looked directly at the Earl. 'I must admit, Papa, that that concerns me too. I'm not suggesting for a moment that if Ben did return we ought to take him back.' That she knew would be just too much for her to bear. 'But I should like to set my mind at rest and be sure that nothing dreadful has happened to him.'

'Very well, child,' his lordship responded gently, betraying once again that he was making a steady recovery from whatever it was that had upset him so much. 'If young Risely is unable to discover anything,

I'll perhaps take a little stroll along to Bow Street.' He glanced up as the door unexpectedly opened. 'Yes, what is it, Cardew?'

The butler came forward bearing a single letter on a silver tray. 'Delivered by hand, my lord, a few minutes ago. The messenger is at this present moment happily refreshing himself in the kitchen, awaiting any response.'

His lordship's grey brows rose as he broke the impressive seal. 'Great heavens!' he exclaimed, after digesting the contents of the brief missive. 'What do you make of that, m'dear?'

Her ladyship cast her eyes over the single sheet written in a bold, elegant hand. 'Perfectly clear,' she answered, betraying none of the evident shock her husband was experiencing. 'His grace the Duke of Sharnbrook has kindly invited us to spend a few days with him at his ancestral home.'

'Yes, but why?' His lordship made a gesture with his hands which betrayed clearly his continuing astonishment. 'The last time I saw young Benedict Risely he was in short coats. Why should he suddenly take it into his head to invite me and my family to Sharnbrook, may I ask?'

The Countess shrugged her shoulders. 'I really have no idea. I can only imagine that Lord Nicholas might possibly have mentioned his friendship with Sophia, and of her kindness in attending their aged aunt's birthday party. Perhaps his grace wishes to thank her in person.'

'Well, I hope that's all it is, and that he ain't taken some foolish notion into his head that our little Sophie would make him the ideal wife.' Far from annoyed, his lordship appeared genuinely amused. 'He'll quickly discover his mistake, if I do take it into my head to accept, and he finds himself having to play host to perhaps the only young filly in the country who has an aversion for titled gentlemen!'

'Do I infer correctly from that that you are undecided whether to accept or not, Papa?' Sophia remarked, her own sense of humour surprisingly rising to the surface. 'You do surprise me! I would have thought you would have grasped such a golden opportunity with both hands. After all, I rather like Lord Nicholas, so there's every chance I should like the brother equally well. Stranger things have happened, you know.'

Rising to her feet, she went over to the door. 'I should accept if I were you. Even if the Duke and I take each other in dislike on sight, a brief spell away from the stale town air will undoubtedly do us all the world of good,' and with that she left the room, and her father gaping after her in open-mouthed astonishment.

No matter what the underlying reason for encouraging her father to accept the unexpected invitation, and she wasn't so very certain herself what it had been, Sophia experienced no regrets whatsoever when Trapp, three days later, tooled the carriage expertly round the sweep of the drive, and she caught her first glimpse of the Duke of Sharnbrook's ancestral home.

Set amid acres of unspoiled parkland, and bathed in mellow late afternoon sunshine, the Restoration mansion, designed by none other than Inigo Jones's famous disciple, was a truly awe-inspiring sight. Sophia could not recall ever having seen anything quite so perfectly situated, and could only wonder at the present head of the family remaining away from such a beautiful spot for such a long time. If it were hers she would never wish to leave the place for five weeks, let alone five years, she felt sure, alighting with the assistance of the liveried footman who had emerged from the eastern entrance of the house the instant Trapp had brought the carriage to a halt.

The interior was no less impressive; at least what she could glimpse of it swiftly earned Sophia's full approval as she, together with her mother and father, followed the elderly housekeeper up an ornately carved oak staircase. At the top they turned left and went along a passageway which led to the recently added east wing. Here Sophia was shown into a bright, airy bedchamber, where hand-painted Chinese paper decorated the walls, and rich green silk hangings adorned both windows and four-poster bed.

She took a moment to stare about her in wonder, from ornately plasterworked ceiling to richly carpeted floor. For more than two centuries, according to the Earl, some of the very best architects and designers had been employed to work on the house and its grounds, creating a place of timeless beauty which rivalled, many considered, the very best in the land.

No mansion she had ever visited before had succeeded in capturing her interest in quite the same way. She did not know what it was about the place that enthralled her so, but she suddenly experienced an overwhelming desire to see it all, to explore every last nook and cranny and uncover its every hidden secret. Consequently, she wasted no time in changing from her travel-creased garments into one of her pretty light muslin day dresses, snatching up a light fringed shawl, and going along to her mother's room.

One glance at the Countess, relaxing on the *chaise-longue* by the open window, was sufficient to inform her that for the present her mother did not share her enthusiasm. 'Oh, I'm sorry, Mama, for barging in this way. Were you asleep?'

'No, child, merely resting my eyes.' She held out her hand, inviting her daughter to sit beside her, and could see at once that there appeared an extra sparkle in those green eyes, something which, she suddenly realised, had been singularly lacking in recent days. 'You seem excited, child. Is it the prospect of meeting our host which has touched your cheeks with added colour, I wonder?' she quizzed. 'He is reputed to be very handsome, you know.'

'Yes, so I'm reliably informed,' Sophia responded drily, thereby betraying her total lack of interest. 'I'm in far more danger of becoming entranced with this glorious house than with its master, I assure you. Have you ever seen a place so perfectly situated?'

'No, I do not believe so.' The Countess, watching her daughter move across to the window, was reminded of something which had occurred to her as rather strange a few days before and, after nodding dismissal to the maid, did not hesitate in attempting to have her curiosity satisfied now.

'Why did I encourage Papa to accept the invitation

to visit here?' Sophia echoed. 'I suppose I considered it would benefit him to get away from town for a few days. I hope the change will do him good. He seems so much better of late, don't you think?'

'Yes, child, I do.' A moment's silence, then, 'Are you sure there was no other reason?'

Sophia closed her eyes, successfully checking the threat of tears which she only ever permitted to fall at night in the privacy of her bedchamber, where she would sob long and silently into her pillow and wake in the morning feeling not a whit the better for having done so. The bouts of weeping might be gradually diminishing; the heartache remained precisely the same, a painful reminder that life could be cruel, and Fate a vicious tormentor for ensuring her path would cross that of a man whom she could not fail to love, but whom she could never hope to marry.

'There were several, Mama,' she admitted softly. 'I was secretly hoping that Lord Nicholas would still be here. Unfortunately, as you probably heard the housekeeper remark after I had enquired, his lordship returned to London this morning.' She shrugged. 'But, no matter. I can see him on our return to town. In the meantime I am determined to enjoy the fresh country air. It will be pleasant to be away from the capital's noise and smells.'

Her ladyship did not doubt that her daughter was being perfectly truthful as far as it went, but she suspected that there was much Sophia was keeping to herself. She refrained from probing further, however, and merely said, 'I sincerely trust we all benefit from this short sojourn in the country, child. But I think I should point out that by encouraging your father to accept Sharnbrook's totally unexpected invitation, you have in all probability put the notion of you achieving a truly splendid match into his head.'

There was a faint reckless quality in Sophia's shout of laughter. 'Well, and why not?'

'Because by your own admission you prefer footmen to marquises.' Her ladyship could not resist reminding her, and then smiled at the astounded expression. 'Yes, I did hear the rumour on the evening of our very own ball,' she admitted, 'and had a fairly shrewd idea from where it had sprung.'

'That I could ever have uttered anything so idiotic!' Sophia exclaimed, utterly ashamed. 'How you have put up with my foolishness all these years, Mama, I shall never know.' A wistful smile tugged at the corner of her mouth. 'Perhaps it has all been a judgement on me, then,' she murmured, hardly aware that she was speaking aloud. 'No more than I deserved.'

The Countess, suddenly alert, detected a look in her daughter's eyes that she had never seen there before. 'What is it, child?' She began to fear the worse. 'Is there something wrong?'

'When we first arrived in London, Mama,' Sophia answered, turning away to stare out of the window at the vast area of parkland, as though seeking solace there, 'I recall Papa was concerned that I should not fall prey to some fortune-hunter. I don't suppose that he ever considered for a moment that his precious daughter might turn out to be the one found wanting, the one who could not quite meet the necessary requirements to make her the perfect wife.'

Turning her back on the magnificent view, she moved swiftly across to the door, fearing that that iron self-control was beginning to show signs of strain. 'Oh, if only frogs could turn into princes!' she cried. 'Well, I cannot have my frog, Mama, so I must be prepared to settle for second best. A duke would suit me as well as any, I suppose.' And before her mother could gather her scattered wits together sufficiently to enquire what on earth she had meant, Sophia had left the room.

For several minutes her ladyship, prey to tumult of conjecture, sat perfectly still, staring in dawning wonder at the closed door, then she flew into the adjoining room to discover her husband, himself standing before one of the tall windows, hands clasped behind his back, contemplating the magnificent views.

'Thomas, we must leave here at once!' she announced, not mincing words.

'Eh…?' Startled out of his reverie, the Earl turned to see his normally placid wife pacing the room like some demented creature. 'Deuce take it, we've only just arrived! What ails you, Marissa?'

'Nothing. But I very much fear Sophia is ailing. And I also very much fear that if Sharnbrook makes her an offer, she'll accept him!'

This was music to his lordship's ears. 'Well, and what of it? It would be a splendid match.'

'Not if she's breaking her heart over her frog, it won't.'

'Frog…?' His lordship's jaw dropped perceptively. 'What the deuce are you talking about, Marissa?' He cast her a sympathetic smile. 'I tell you what it is, old girl. All that gadding about in London has over-tired you, has been a bit of a strain. You need a rest.'

'There's nothing at all the matter with me!' she snapped, for perhaps the first time ever coming perilously close to losing her temper. 'It's Sophia you should be concerned about.' She ceased her pacing. 'I should have realised. I detected the changes in her…knew someone was exerting a beneficial influence…But I never imagined for a moment that she was falling in love…God, what a fool I've been!'

'Fallen in love? Sophia…? With whom, pray?' His lordship was utterly bewildered now. 'With the possible exception of young Risely, she ain't shown a ha'p'orth of interest in any man since we arrived in town, as far as I'm aware.'

'No, I know she hasn't,' her ladyship agreed, concern clearly writ across her pale features. 'And that is precisely what worries me, for I very much fear she has lost her heart to—to someone you would find totally unacceptable.'

'Ha! So that's the way of it, is it!' His lordship bellowed, bringing his fist down none too gently on a conveniently positioned occasional table. 'I might have guessed the little minx would do something like this just to annoy me.'

'If you truly believe that, Thomas, then you do our daughter a grave injustice,' her ladyship countered, surprising her husband out of his ill-humour, and swiftly gaining his full attention. 'If you had not been so wrapped up in your own misery, so uninterested in most everything that was going on about you of late, except your own private concerns, you could not

have failed to perceive the changes in Sophia. She
has dealt with your megrims and unreasonable behaviour with such a wealth of patience and understanding
that I have felt proud to be her mother. Not once did
she come even remotely close to losing her temper
when you foolishly paraded every buck and dandy
you could find before her. And little wonder the poor
child remained totally unimpressed with all those can-
didates you found for her hand, when her feelings
were engaged already!'

'Yes, but who is this man, may I ask?' the Earl
demanded, not unreasonably.

'I don't know!' Striving to maintain her composure, the Countess seated herself in the nearest chair,
and took a moment or two to try to make some sense
of her disordered thoughts. 'If I had not been so concerned about you in recent weeks, I might have been
more observant where Sophia was concerned.
Evidently she's taken great pains to keep the truth
from me. Perhaps, in her heart of hearts, she has
known all along that by marrying this man she would
be making a great *mésalliance*.'

Raising her head, she looked across the room at the
Earl who was looking no longer angry, just merely
thoughtful. 'In truth, Thomas, I do not know what has
been taking place right under our very noses during
these past weeks. The only thing I'm certain of is that
our only daughter is desperately unhappy and striving
not to betray her feelings to anyone. If there is a possibility that a marriage to this unknown man who has
won our daughter's affections could take place, are
you prepared to sit back and permit her to marry

someone whom she could never love merely to please you?'

A long silence, then, 'No, Marissa I am not.' There was no mistaking the old steely determination in his voice. 'Come, let us find our daughter, and discover precisely what has been going on!'

Sophia, blissfully unaware that both her parents were in hot pursuit, was at that present moment walking along the gravel paths at the back of the mansion, and rapidly coming to the conclusion that the strain of the past few days was finally beginning to take its toll. Not only had she come perilously close to breaking down in front of her mother, but now she was convinced her eyes were playing tricks on her, for she had just seen someone who, had she not known better, she could have sworn was none other than her old groom Clem Claypole, mounted on the most magnificent black, heading in the direction of the stable block.

'Unutterable madness!' she muttered, entering a huge conservatory and finding herself amid garlands of fragrant blooms, most of which she did not recognise.

Finding the humidity a little oppressive, but the heady scent quite delightful, she stood for a moment gazing in wonder at the wonderful exotic collection, before focusing her attention on a tall specimen in a huge terracotta pot just a few feet away.'

'Be careful with that,' a beautifully modulated and startlingly familiar voice warned, as Sophia stretched out tentative fingers to touch one leathery, ovate leaf.

'It has travelled a very long way. From the Carolinas to be precise. It is the only specimen on the estate, and so is being treated with the utmost care.'

'Quite understandable,' Sophia responded, quickly withdrawing her hand as though she feared it might get burned, and then turning sharply to see a tall, immaculately attired figure emerge from between the dense foliage. The fact that some detached part of her brain had instantly recognised something achingly familiar in the deep voice should have been sufficient warning, and yet she still found herself gaping like a half-wit when she raised her eyes to see that beloved face, now clean-shaven, and with its crowning golden mane cut to a more acceptable length, smiling down at her.

'Ben!' she gasped, still reluctant to believe the evidence of her own eyes, as she took in every detail of the faultless attire: the well-starched cravat, which despite the humidity managed to retain its crispness, the expensive linen shirt tucked into the waistband of tight-fitting breeches, and the black-leather top-boots with their looking-glass shine. What he was doing here and dressed like a gentleman were the first of many questions amassing in her poor throbbing head, but before she could begin her inquiry an interruption occurred, and she found herself gaping yet again at the equally familiar figure who suddenly appeared in the doorway.

'Clem,' she murmured faintly, wondering if she were truly running mad.

'Hello, my lady. It is good to see you again.' Her ex-groom's lopsided grin faded as he turned to his new master standing directly behind her. 'I'm sorry for the intrusion, your grace, but would you be wanting Sultan saddled again today?'

'No, not today, Clem. I envisage my time will be fully occupied with—er—other and more important matters.'

Even in her hopelessly confused state, where she refused to face the one fact that was becoming patently obvious, Sophia could not fail to detect the note of amusement in that well-remembered, beloved voice.

'By the by, has Trapp recovered from the shock of coming face to face with me yet? I hope you've taken good care of him.'

'He's sharing my room above the stable, your grace. We'll perhaps have a tankard or two of ale later and talk over old times.' Clem chuckled. 'Never fear, your grace, he'll be as right as rain by morning.'

Somehow managing to respond to her ex-groom's farewell, Sophia remained staring fixedly at the spot he had just vacated. 'I know this is going to sound incredibly foolish,' she said with dangerous restraint, 'but why did Clem refer to you as your grace?'

A brief silence, then: 'All my employees grant me that courtesy,' Benedict responded softly. He could almost hear those tiny white teeth grinding together, and wanted nothing more than to take her into his arms and kiss away the rising anger before there was the understandable explosion of wrath, but he remained resolutely standing those few feet away.

'I know how you must be feeling at this precise moment—hurt, angry, perhaps a little foolish for not having guessed the truth long ago. Maybe even bitterly resentful because you believe I've been playing some May game at your expense.'

All those things and more, she thought, but said, somehow still maintaining that admirable self-control of which her mother had become so justifiably proud, 'Well…and haven't you?'

'No, my darling. From the start I've been in deadly earnest, wanting only to get to know you a good deal better.'

She did turn to look at him then, and he held the openly sceptical gaze levelly, instinctively knowing what she must be thinking and feeling, and not blaming her in the least for the contempt he saw mirrored in those lovely green eyes. 'I'll own, I did not go about achieving my objective in the most sensible way. In fact, it was damnably foolish of me to pose as a groom.'

'So why did you do it?' she put in, nowhere near ready to believe him yet, nor forgive him, either, for that matter.

'Because of something Nicholas had mentioned about you—about your aversion to titled gentlemen, and because…Oh, I don't know!' He ran impatient fingers through his hair, still annoyed with himself, if the truth were known, for embarking on such tomfoolery in the first place. 'I suppose because I gave way to a moment's sheer irresponsibility, a desire to enjoy just one last madcap venture before I took upon my shoulders the huge responsibility of becoming the head of the noble Risely family. God only knows what madness possessed me! I knew I couldn't hope to maintain the pretence for very long.'

His sigh was so heartfelt that she could not fail to be moved by it. She regarded him in silence, realising in those moments what ought to have been abundantly clear to her from the start—that he was every bit as much in love with her as she was with him. Did anything else really matter?

'I love you, Sophia Cleeve—have done so from the first moment I set eyes on you that morning in Bond Street,' he freely admitted, which merely confirmed what she now knew in her heart of hearts to be true. There was a great deal more she needed to know, but she was prepared to wait. All that mattered was that he was here now.

Something in her expression gave her away, and he was not slow to hold out his hand. 'Will you be my Duchess?'

'Yes,' she answered, willingly surrendering her fingers. 'But only because I intend to spend the rest of my life making you suffer unimaginable torments for the abominable trick you have played upon me!'

His triumphant shout of laughter was muffled in a tender embrace that dispensed with the need for further explanations. They clung to each other, exchanging kiss for kiss, caress for caress, until a staunchly disapproving voice demanding to know what the deuce was going on brought them down from the heady heights of their mutual passion with a jolt, and they fell apart half amused, half shamefaced to see the Earl glowering at them from the doorway, and the Countess looking not just a little confused as well.

'Loath though I am to contradict you on anything, Marissa, but I feel your reading of the situation in this instance is grossly inaccurate,' said his lordship ominously. 'Far from suffering a broken heart, it would seem our daughter is fast becoming a trollop!'

Sophia's only response to this unflattering assessment of her morals was to burst out laughing, and it was left to Benedict to take charge of the delicate situation. Suggesting that his future wife escort her mother back to the house, and arrange for a tea-tray to be brought to the yellow salon, he set about soothing his future father-in-law's ruffled feathers which he did so successfully that his lordship's laughing comment on first rejoining the ladies was, 'My dear Marissa, does it all not make you feel incredibly old? Our groom of all things!'

'Not at all,' she responded, bubbling with mirth herself. 'My only concern is that the gossips will get to learn about it all.'

'I took great pains to ensure that I wasn't recognised,' Benedict assured her. 'But in the unlikely event that someone did penetrate my disguise, I suggest a quiet engagement here at Sharnbrook, which can easily be arranged in a very few days. The Ton will then believe that it was a clear case of love at first sight...Which, of course, is no less than the truth.' He went across to Sophia. 'Are you agreeable to a swift engagement, my love?'

Her glowing smile was answer enough. She was more than happy to fall in with any plans he wished to make, which included a Christmas wedding to be held in the tiny church at Abbot Giles. The Countess was slightly disappointed, for she had dreamed of a truly magnificent wedding for her only daughter.

'It is what they both want, my dear,' his lordship remarked, watching the happy couple wander out on to the terrace a short time later. 'They can, as Sophia suggested, do all the lavish celebrating and entertaining they wish to when they go to London next spring.'

'Yes, of course they can. And I mustn't forget that dear Beatrice and Harry's wedding was a truly charming affair. I see no reason why Sophia's shouldn't be too. They're very much in love, that's plain to see.' She drew her attention away from the glowingly happy couple to glance up at her husband's profile. 'You must be overjoyed by the turn of events.'

'Very,' he assured her, then with an abrupt change of subject said, 'I shall return to London after the party, and arrange for a notice of the engagement to be placed in the newspapers. I see little point in remaining in town until the end of the Season, so I shall return to Jaffrey House at the beginning of June.'

'You mean you won't be returning here?' She was both surprised and disappointed. 'But you heard me promise Benedict that I would remain here with Sophia for several weeks.'

'And so you shall, my dear.' The Earl drew her arm through his. 'It is just that there are one or two matters requiring my attention which I have left unresolved for far too long. Nothing for you to concern yourself about.'

Her ladyship was not so certain, but kept this reflection to herself, and merely allowed him to lead her out on to the terrace to rejoin their daughter and future son-in-law...

MILLS & BOON®

Makes any time special™

Mills & Boon publish 29 new titles every month. Select from...

Modern Romance™   Tender Romance™

Sensual Romance™

Medical Romance™ Historical Romance™

MAT2

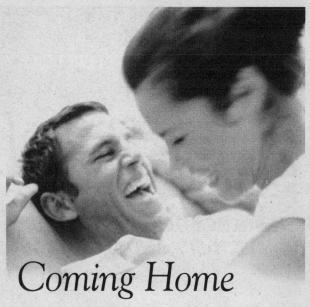

Coming Home

Scandal drove David away
Now love will draw him home . . .

PENNY JORDAN

Published 21st September